www.HarperLin.com

Chocolat Chaud Murder

A Patisserie Mystery
Book #9

by Harper Lin

ISBN-13: 978-1987859294

ISBN-10: 1987859294

Contents

Recipes

Chapter 1

Clémence wasn't one of those girls who grew up dreaming about her wedding day. She always thought she would get married but she never quite understood what all the fuss was about when it came to the wedding planning, or why it took some people more than a year to get ready for the big day.

The one thing that did cause her a bit of stress was finding a beautiful wedding dress. The dress was crucial. Not that beautiful wedding dresses were in short supply in Paris, but she needed to find *her* perfect dress. Once she did, she was sure the rest of the wedding would snowball into place.

Clémence felt she was close. At La Belle, a small boutique in the 6th arrondissement, she'd already tried on six gorgeous white dresses. If only she could make up her mind. The problem was she was trying on dresses alone.

After wolfing down a quick lunch at Damour, the flagship store of her family's patisserie chain, she'd hailed a cab to her appointment. On an early Wednesday afternoon, all her friends were at work. Celine, who worked as a hostess at Damour, was supposed to come with her, but another hostess had called in sick, and Celine had to cover for her. Without a friend by her side, Clémence didn't have an objective second opinion.

The first three dresses she'd been drawn to were all classic strapless styles. The fourth had a ball gown skirt, and the fifth and sixth were more daring designs with corset waists. One of the corsets was encrusted with diamonds. She didn't have the budget for a dress like that, but at the urgency of Eva Vincent, the salesgirl, she'd tried it on for fun.

Eva insisted she looked great, but Clémence felt a little ridiculous, as if she were a fairy godmother with a bit of showgirl thrown in. She figured she would probably end up with one of the classic styles. She usually preferred modest clothing. Her clothes, considered stylish by most people, were all classic pieces, similar to what every other girl in Paris wore—tailored basics that were so tasteful, they were almost boring.

Even though she was an heiress to Damour, Clémence shied away from attention. She represented the Damour family brand sometimes and had attended events with her parents since she was a teenager. Once the media had gotten wind of her socialite status, she had been a fixture in the entertainment sections of papers and blogs until she'd abandoned everything to travel the world. She'd returned to Paris less than a year ago, where she had slowly gotten her life back together.

After she'd come back, she'd been a bit hesitant to oversee the family business while her parents spent time in Asia to open more patisseries, but she'd learned to embrace her leadership skills and public exposure. Sometimes, the exposure was for other reasons—getting mixed up with the police while solving murder mysteries, for example—but that was another story.

She had always been uncomfortable with people staring at her. She hoped she would feel differently at her wedding. If she had her way, she would elope with Arthur to a tiny church in the countryside and avoid all the usual theatrics, but she couldn't. In essence, a wedding seemed to be a celebration for everyone else, and the couple had to put on the show, especially to please their families.

Meeting the man she was going to marry was the best thing that had happened in the past year. Their love story began as the typical love-hate relationship often found in romantic comedies. Clémence had laughed when she'd told Eva the story of how she had started dating Arthur. He had been right under her nose the entire time. Quite literally. He'd lived two floors below her family's apartment in the 16th arrondissement.

She'd always thought of him as an arrogant playboy, a finance guy who was a total bore. Yet the more she got to know him, the more she fell in love with him.

Their mothers had wanted the two of them to date before they'd known they liked each other, and the women would have a fit if she and Arthur didn't get married in a proper ceremony. Arthur was also very private and low-key, but he'd been more enthused about wedding planning than she'd thought he would be. He'd already selected his suit and helped her choose the invitations.

Arthur's mother had generously suggested using her house in Normandy as a venue, and Clémence might just agree to it. The house was really a mansion, with an even bigger garden. It was the perfect size for the seventy guests she planned to invite. Compared with other weddings Clémence had attended, hers was going to be small and intimate. She wanted the experience to be as laid back as possible.

Finding the right dress was the most stressful part of the process so far but also the most fun.

After changing back into one of the three strapless dresses for a second look, Clémence asked Eva, "Can I take a photo of myself in the dress? I want to show my friends."

Eva, a pretty brunette in her early thirties, shook her head apologetically. "I'm sorry. The owners have a strict no-photo policy."

"Really? Why is that?"

"I don't know why exactly. I think Adine, the designer, just doesn't like it."

La Belle was an intimate boutique tucked into one of the small cobblestone streets. The showroom was as big as one of the many antique bookstores in the same neighborhood. No one else had an appointment at that time, and Clémence was the only customer in the store. The experience had been quite peaceful. She wouldn't begrudge the designer for wanting to keep the shopping experience a low-key affair. After all, if she had created the most beautiful wedding dresses, she could set whatever rule she wanted at her store.

"I like all of them," Clémence said. "Well, these four most of all. Can you help me note down which styles they are so that I can come back with friends later this week to look at them again?"

"Of course." The young woman's business-like expression cracked when she smiled. "It's difficult to make a choice with such lovely options, isn't it?"

"It really is. Adine is so talented. Can I ask for your honest opinion? Which one of these dresses did you like better on me?"

Taking the matter seriously, Eva scrutinized the five dresses on the racks and the one Clémence was wearing. "You were obviously not comfortable in the corset styles. I noticed when you were wearing them, so I think you were right to dismiss them. You looked like you couldn't even move properly in them."

"True," Clémence agreed. "Comfort takes precedence over style for me, to tell you the truth. You can take away the corset options, then. At least I went out of my comfort zone and tried them on, right?"

"I'll give you points for that," Eva said. "The ball gown made you look too much like Cinderella, but I sense you're not the princess type."

Clémence laughed. "I'm glad to hear that. Yes, the dress is a bit too fluffy for me. Actually, I threw that in for my mother's sake. She wanted me to be in something 'fit for royalty.' But you're right. This isn't me. I'm looking for something simple and chic. What do you think of this one?" She gestured to the one she was wearing—a simple ivory silk dress with a skirt that flowed and draped around the floor.

"The strapless styles are lovely, but maybe too boring." Eva seemed more comfortable speaking frankly now.

"Really?" Clémence frowned. "Even if I were to put on the accessories?"

"I don't mean to insult you. These dresses are great. You would look beautiful in whatever you wore. It's just that it's your special day. You may want to stand out more, even just a little. Wait." Eva abruptly turned and walked to the back, where she began flipping through one of the racks. "You overlooked this one." She held out a dress inside a plastic cover. "I know you weren't looking for lace, but I think this would look great on you."

"Lace?" Clémence's face fell. "I wasn't." She didn't want to look like a doily.

"What do you have to lose? Just try it on. It's simple enough, and it's romantic."

After Eva opened the plastic, Clémence fingered the delicate lace. The style wasn't strapless, as she'd wanted, but it looked as though it would hug her body even tighter than the strapless styles.

She hesitated. "It's rather low in the front. The neckline is, well, rather plunging."

"Don't worry." Eva gave a dismissive wave. "You won't look provocative because you don't have a big bust. Go on. Try it."

"All right," Clémence said with doubt in her voice. But Eva was right. What did she have to lose?

When Clémence emerged from the dressing room, she was surprised how good she looked. Even though the neckline was much lower than the other dresses she'd tried on, the dress still looked classy and elegant on her. The silhouette showed off her body in a feminine way, and the lace hugged her like a glove.

"What do you think?" Eva tried to sound indifferent, but Clémence could tell she was eager for a favorable answer by the way she arched her eyebrows.

Clémence broke into a wide smile. "I love it. It's actually really comfortable."

"Good." Eva grinned back. "I'm rarely wrong."

"You're good at your job. I could make a rash decision and buy it on the spot, but I'm still going to bring at least one friend in for a second opinion."

"Of course. This is not a light decision. I'll keep your size available in the back."

"Merci. Thanks so much for all your help today."

"No problem." Eva grinned again. "I love my job."

After Clémence changed out of the dress, she heard a loud scream. She was still zipping her jeans up when she stumbled out of the changing room to see what the commotion was.

Eva was at the rear of the store in front of the open back door. A young woman stood at the door. She looked to be about twenty-five, with wavy, long reddish-brown hair, and she looked as pale as a ghost.

"What happened?" Eva asked her.

"She's dead!" the young woman cried.

Chapter 2

"Who's dead?" Clémence asked.

"Adine," the woman cried.

Clémence gasped. "The designer?"

"How?" Eva asked incredulously. "Perrie, are you sure?"

Clémence walked over to the women and gently guided Perrie to sit in one of the cushioned chairs by the wall. The young woman put her head in her hands. "I can't believe this is real. I saw blood everywhere!"

"Call the police," Clémence said to Eva before turning back to Perrie. "Tell me what happened, please."

Perrie slowly spoke. "I was looking for Adine in the *atelier*, but she wasn't there, so I went up to her apartment. The door was open. I called her name. She didn't answer, so I looked for her. She was on the floor, and—oh, it was quite the sight. Like in those gruesome murder mystery shows, except this was real."

Perrie was shaking as Eva put her phone away after making the call.

"Wait, so Adine lives upstairs?" Clémence asked.

"Yes," Eva said. "There's an atelier on the second floor, where she works and makes all of the dresses by hand with a couple of other seamstresses."

No wonder these dresses cost a fortune, Clémence thought.

"She also lives on the third floor," Eva continued, "in her private apartment."

"So the store, the atelier, and the apartment are all connected?" Clémence asked.

Perrie nodded. "Just think of it as one big house."

"And who are you, may I ask?"

"I'm Adine's assistant. I've only been working for her for a month."

"I need to see the crime scene," Clémence said.

"Shouldn't you wait for the police to do that?" Eva asked.

"I work with the police," Clémence blurted out without thinking.

Eva turned to her in surprise. "Really?" She paused. "You don't look like a police officer."

Clémence didn't exactly lie. She had worked with the police numerous times. She was on a first-name basis with them, even if the head inspector wanted to forget hers. "I work with the police on a consultant basis." That was also not a lie. She was similar to a consultant, even if the police never paid her for her good work.

"Consulting on... murders?" Eva asked.

"Yes."

"But you're not a detective."

"No."

"Like Sherlock Holmes," Perrie said, brightening up a little. "That's what he does!"

Clémence had to chuckle. "I'm nowhere near as clever as Sherlock. I can't tell what happened to someone just by scratches on a wall."

"So what can you do?" Eva asked, curiosity shining in her bright, green eyes.

"This whole thing is crazy," Perrie said, "but I want to know too."

"Why don't you lead the way," Clémence said to Perrie, "and I'll show you?"

"All right." Perrie stood up reluctantly. "You first, though. I have the keys, but the door is probably still open. I don't think I even want to go up there with you."

"Okay. That's fine. Eva, can you stay here to talk to the police when they get here?"

"Sure."

This wasn't Clémence's first rodeo. She'd seen plenty of dead bodies up close and personal, and she could remember when she had once been squeamish about them like Perrie was. Clémence was still a little squeamish, but at least she didn't feel the vomit rising in her throat anymore.

Perrie looked pale. Clémence didn't know if it was because she was a redhead and naturally had paper-white skin, or because she wanted to puke.

Perrie led Clémence through the back door of the store, which was a small space with an employees' restroom, a closet, and a staircase. They went up the stairs.

The door to the atelier was open, and Clémence looked in. The space was beautiful, with floral wallpaper and big, bright windows. A row of mannequins lined one wall, half cloaked in beautiful completed wedding dresses, and half in a state of undress.

White fabric samples were scattered over one of three tables. Chairs and workspaces suggested that at least three people could occupy the space.

"There are the stairs going up to the apartment." Perrie pointed to a black iron spiral staircase in one corner of the atelier.

Before she went up, Clémence wanted to question Perrie. How did she know Perrie didn't do it? After all, that was what the police were going to investigate. A quick glance at Perrie told her the girl hadn't been in contact with any blood. She wore a nude-colored coat, so any blood splatters would be obvious.

"Did you see Adine today before she was found, you know, up there?" Clémence asked.

"Yes. I was with her this morning in the atelier. Nobody else was at the atelier. The two seam-stresses aren't here this week. They're sisters, and they both went back to their hometown in Italy for an aunt's birthday. I was alone in the atelier most of the time, working on my laptop. Adine was here from time to time, designing, but she was distract-ed today. She went out to smoke a lot. I went out for a late lunch because I had so much work to catch up with. I was gone for about an hour. When I came back, I found Adine up there, dead."

"I see. You didn't touch anything, right?"

Perrie balked. "That depends. I'm here all the time. I touch everything!"

"Even the things in her apartment?"

"No, I don't get invited up there so much, but I touched the doorknob when I was trying to find her. Oh my gosh! Do you think the police will think I had something to do with it?"

"Well, they'll question you," Clémence said. "I think you'll be okay because you're innocent."

Perrie breathed a sigh of relief. "Thanks for believing me." Perrie looked at her. "Why do you believe me?"

"I just do." Clémence didn't add that she'd been in the same situation before. Just because someone found a body didn't mean she had anything to do with the murder. It would be pretty stupid for a real killer to do that. Most people were not great actors.

"Do me a favor," Clémence said.

"Sure," Perrie said. "What is it?"

"Say you're my witness."

"Witness for what?"

"Tell the police that I didn't touch anything. That I didn't tamper with any evidence."

"I thought you worked with the police," Perrie said.

"I do. But the head inspector has it in for me. He hates that I'm always solving his cases."

"Okay." Perrie shrugged. "If you can put in a good word for me and, you know, stop me from being arrested for murder."

Clémence lightly shook her head. "If we're talking about Cyril St. Clair, it won't matter what I say. He's going to be nasty. Get ready for it."

"This is going to be a long day, isn't it?" Perrie asked.

Clémence walked up the iron staircase. The door was still ajar, so she put the sleeve of her black sweater over her fingers and pushed it open. She didn't want her DNA on anything.

Luckily, she didn't have to go far into the apartment to see the body.

First, she noticed the door's lock had not been tampered with. Whoever went in must have been someone Adine knew. Unless...

"Hey, Perrie," Clémence called down to the nervous young lady.

"Yes?"

"When you went for lunch, did the door lock behind you?"

"Yes. It locks automatically."

"I thought so," Clémence said. "So the door to the atelier was definitely locked?"

"Yes. Unless Adine left it open for some reason, but she wouldn't do that. She doesn't like to be disturbed by anyone downstairs."

"What about the apartment door?"

"I don't know. Maybe. When Adine talks on the phone, and the conversation is one she wants to keep private, she goes up to her room. She does keep the door closed. I'm assuming the door is also one that locks automatically."

"It is." Clémence recognized the lock. It was a common lock in Paris, and it was sturdy enough that the door couldn't be pushed open once it was closed. Someone would need a key if they wanted to lock the deadbolt and truly secure it. If it hadn't been locked with a key, someone could use something extremely thin but durable, like a strip of X-ray film, and slide it in between the door and the frame to open it. If a murderer were that meticulous to bring a strip of X-ray film to the murder scene however, he or she probably wouldn't have bashed in Adine's head quite so obviously.

The blood was pooling around the woman's body. She was face down, so Clémence couldn't see her face. Adine was wearing a white turtleneck sweater, which made the blood look even more gruesome.

Her apartment had a lot of natural light. The sun poured in, making the scene look cheery in a creepy way.

The window faced the side of another building that probably contained apartments, but the windows on the building were shut. With all the sunlight that morning, it would have been difficult for the neighbors to see into Adine's window. Most people were probably at work at that time of day anyhow.

Time was ticking. The police would be there any second. Clémence looked around, gathering whatever she could in her mind.

The killer had a small time frame, only an hour or so during Perrie's lunch break. The person had gotten in—or Adine had let him or her in—then the killer had gone up to the apartment and had struck Adine with a lamp. Clémence saw the lamp lying on the floor. That type of crime probably happened in the heat of the moment, with no forethought from the killer.

If the killer were smart enough, perhaps he'd wiped the fingerprints on the lamp clean, but maybe not. The police would handle that.

After the attack, the killer could have easily fled down the stairs and back out the door without anyone in the boutique noticing.

Clémence sighed. This was going to be a long day indeed.

Chapter 3

"Of course *you* would be here," Inspector Cyril St. Clair said to her.

Clémence had returned to the boutique just minutes before the police had arrived. Another bride and her two girlfriends had come for their appointment, but Eva had politely turned them away, citing an emergency. The bride had been furious, saying she'd come all the way from Issy-les-Moulineaux, a suburb of Paris, and she'd demanded more information. Eva told her a tenant on the top floor had passed away, but she didn't go into the details, such as the deceased was the dress designer and she had been murdered. The bride had rescheduled her appointment and left in a huff.

It was a good thing La Belle had no more appointments for the rest of the day and that the store was located on a side street, because when the police arrived, they were not on display for the general public to see. Two police cars parked directly in front of the store, followed by Cyril's comically small car.

Clémence had watched from the window as he emerged from the driver's seat as if he were coming out of a clown car. Cyril was so tall and wiry that it was a wonder he could even fit inside the car. When he saw her, he'd scowled.

"Shouldn't you be congratulating me?" Clémence asked him. "I'm getting married, you know."

Cyril gave a slow clap. "How happy for you, but I'm not sure if congratulations are in order for this fiancé of yours. So, have you found a dress?"

Clémence crossed her arms, as if anticipating the annoying banter that was coming. "Possibly."

"And the dress designer happens to be dead? On the same day?"

"Yes."

"Was she eating one your macarons or croissants or whatever?"

She sighed. "Shouldn't you be doing your job instead of berating a customer?"

"Funny how you always happen to be at ninety-nine point nine percent of Paris's murder crime scenes. It has crossed my mind more than once that you're the mastermind behind all these murders, you know."

"It's obvious that little crosses your mind, so I applaud you for having at least a little bit of brain activity going on. Even if you're dead wrong and completely crazy."

"Sir?" One of Cyril's colleagues leaned in to whisper in his ear.

Without saying another word to her, Cyril went to the back of the store and probably up to Adine's apartment, the crime scene.

Clémence sat down and watched Cyril's new partner grill Perrie.

Eva was going to be questioned soon, and so was she. In fact, they would probably spend more time with the police than they really cared to.

Eva was sitting on a couch by the wall on which customers' friends usually sat when waiting for the bride to come out of a changing room in potential dresses.

Clémence sat next to her. "This sucks, huh?"

"It's absolutely crazy. Did you discover anything?" Eva asked. "Who murdered Adine?"

"I don't know, unfortunately. I need to know more about Adine. It must be someone who knew her. Were you friends with Adine?"

"I wouldn't exactly call us friends. She's my boss. We respect her."

"We?"

"Yes. Me and another saleswoman, Laurie. It's her day off today."

"I'm very sorry about Adine. It must be hard. Who would hate her enough to do this to her?"

"I don't know," Eva said. She thought about it. "I guess you could say that Adine was a bit temperamental."

"Did she have a lot of enemies?"

"Maybe. Her assistants never lasted for long. Adine can be demanding, a bit stubborn. I can't imagine who would hate her enough to murder her, but she wasn't a ray of sunshine."

"Who else did she spend a lot of time with?"

"Well, there's our other boss, Jennifer Moss. She's the co-owner of this place."

"Moss? Doesn't sound French."

"She's British. She met Adine in college when she was in Paris for a semester. Right after they graduated, they went into business together. That was ten years ago."

"Jennifer doesn't live upstairs with Adine? It looks like a pretty big apartment. Big for Paris, anyway."

"I heard that years ago, when they bought this location, they used to share the apartment, yes. Once the shop became successful, Jennifer moved out. She used to joke that Adine was impossible to live with, and if she stayed for another minute, their friendship would've been over."

"How long ago was that?"

"Oh, I don't know. You'll have to ask her."

"And how long have you been working here?"

"About five years. I was one of their first employees. They used to be on the sales floor themselves."

"Sounds like Jennifer must know Adine quite well."

"Yes. They're like an old married couple. They were always arguing. It's probably for the best that Jennifer moved out. I don't think it's a good idea to live with friends. I mean, I used to room with my best friend, and she always left her clothes on the floor and dirty dishes in the sink, and I don't even speak to her anymore because she drove me crazy in the semester we were rooming together."

"Have you heard them fighting recently?"

"Well..." Eva paused to think about it. "I think Jennifer was keen on opening more boutiques. This one is doing quite well. Adine didn't want to, though."

"Why not?"

"Oh, I don't know. I guess she didn't want more work. The dresses are all made up at the atelier. Yup, I think they did fight about that. Jennifer wanted to outsource the dress making, and Adine wanted to keep the boutique the way it was. They couldn't stand each other sometimes." Eva's eyes widened after that slipped out. "Not that I want to insinuate Jennifer's the killer. Friends fight."

"Who do you think could be the killer, then?"

"Well, there's Adine's ex-boyfriend. I've seen him hanging around. He's tall and dark haired, big nose, but handsome in a brooding Louis Garrel kind of way. They've been on and off for months, maybe the past year."

"Who is he?"

Eva shrugged. "I think his name is Noel. I don't know what he does or anything. In fact, he's usually dressed kind of shabbily. I'm surprised he was Adine's type. I just know he was her boyfriend, not much more. I don't have a relationship with Adine where we talk about our personal lives, you know?"

Just then, they were interrupted by Inspector Cyril St. Clair.

"Clémence." He grinned as if he'd caught her red handed. "I knew it. I knew you were responsible for the murder."

"What?" she exclaimed, standing up.

"Maybe not you specifically, but Damour."

Clémence crossed her arms. Not again. *Don't say it.*

"A Damour product was found in our victim's kitchen," he declared proudly.

She moved him away from Eva. She didn't want any rumors spreading about her family's company if she could help it. "Oh, say it loud enough for everyone to hear," she hissed. "What is it this time?"

"We found a jar of Damour's hot chocolate mix in the kitchen."

"So?" Clémence said defensively. "A lot of people have that product in their homes. It's sold everywhere. In fact, it's one of our supermarket bestsellers. Maybe *the* best."

"It just so happens that our victim was drinking your supermarket bestseller before she was killed." Cyril clapped his hands with glee and let out a laugh fit for a hyena.

"So? She likes hot chocolate. It's not like the hot chocolate killed her."

"Maybe not, but it's not a great omen, is it? I wonder why the public hasn't figured out yet that eating anything from Damour will kill them."

"Because it's not true. If you think that's the case, maybe you should lay off on our éclairs."

That shut Cyril up. He enjoyed Damour treats as much as anybody else in Paris. He was obsessed with their chocolate éclairs, and their pistachios too, but he would never admit it to her.

"There are plenty of better éclair places in the city," he finally mumbled.

"Why don't you tell me something useful about the case?" Clémence asked. "If you're lucky, I'll help you, and you might actually get this case solved."

"Your ego is getting the best of you," Cyril said. "Remember what happened when you got over-confident last time."

Clémence shrugged, even though she wanted to cringe. She had accused an innocent suspect and embarrassed her in front of her colleagues. Nobody was perfect. Clémence had been wrong, but she always solved the case in the end.

"I think this is an open-and-shut case," Cyril said. "Her boyfriend did it. The victim had previously reported him and was even considering a restraining order. My colleague tells me she almost went through with it last week. Now I hear this guy was also seen loitering outside the store this morning. Obviously, he snuck upstairs, surprised her in her apartment, they had an argument, and he killed her. We don't need your help this time, Mademoiselle Damour."

"But—"

"That was obviously what happened." Looking self-satisfied, Cyril walked away to bark orders at his team.

Chapter 4

The sun was close to setting. Clémence had told one of Cyril's colleagues everything she knew. She'd left out the part about sneaking up to the apartment to look at the body, however. Not that the experience had been very helpful.

She left Eva and Perrie to the questioning and started heading toward the Seine. The dimming sun cast an orange reflection on the water as she walked and thought about the case. Sure, Cyril had said it was open and shut, but could it be that easy? It was never that easy.

What did she know about the boyfriend? Eva had said Adine had an on-and-off boyfriend. The relationship didn't sound very stable. If Adine really had thought about a restraining order against this Noel guy, he must be dangerous.

After such a crazy day, walking along the river calmed Clémence, so she decided to walk the rest of the way home. All she had to do was walk toward the Eiffel Tower. Her apartment wasn't far from Place du Trocadéro.

She passed the green bookstands along the Seine, where sellers were packing up for the day. They sold antique books, souvenirs, and vintage posters. She used to love poking through those stands as a kid. As an adult, she bought so many books that most of them sat on her bookshelf unread.

She smiled. Paris was a city of nostalgia, romantic to a fault, and even better in memories. Even as she was living in the moment, she felt as if she were lost in time.

Time was a strange thing. That morning, the only thing occupying her mind had been finding the right wedding dress. Then there had been a murder.

And that murder was bothering her. She couldn't stop thinking about it. The police had every reason to believe the killer was the pesky ex-boyfriend, but her instinct told her she needed to investigate further. Had she developed a fondness for solving cases? It could be gratifying, like solving a puzzle, but also extremely frustrating. If she had her way, there would be no murders in Paris—or anywhere.

She decided she would put the case out of her mind. If Cyril really thought he had figured it out, then she would let it be. She was busy... busier than usual. Christmas was coming up, and she had presents to buy. Her parents were moving back to Paris after spending the year in Asia. Her brother, sister, and their families were coming to stay in the apartment for Christmas too. Plus, she had Damour to run. It would be extra busy during the holidays, and she was glad her parents would be there to help. In addition to the flagship store, her family owned a couple of smaller patisseries around Paris that Clémence popped into once in a while to make sure they were all under control.

By the time she reached her apartment, it was nightfall. Even though winter had already descended, the week had been surprisingly mild. She was almost hot when she climbed the stairs to Palais de Chaillot. Her legs also felt rubbery before long. She really needed to join a gym.

For a while, she had been pretty active with those boot camp classes that took place in the Tuileries, but the weather had been warm then, and she'd thought she would get used to the high-intensity workouts. She hadn't. Her thighs had burned for days after the classes, and she had always felt tired. Her diet probably didn't help. She had to ease up on eating on the job. All that butter and sugar was only okay in moderation.

When she got home, Arthur was packing some of his things in boxes.

"Clémence." He gave her a kiss hello. "I went to pick you up from the store, but they said you hadn't been in."

"Long story," she said. "I'll tell you at dinner."

"Did you find a dress?"

"Possibly." She wasn't sure at that point if she really wanted to buy a dress from a murdered designer. "What are you doing?" she asked Arthur. "Are you getting packed up to go already?"

"Your parents are coming home this week. They don't even know I've been living here."

"They have some idea, I think."

"Do they?"

"I'm assuming. It's only natural you're here a lot. After all, your family lives two floors below us, and you have a room upstairs."

"Yes, but I pretty much moved all my stuff in here. I've been squatting." He laughed.

"Oh, you can squat here as much as you want." Clémence gave him a pinch on the cheek.

"Luckily, I don't have a lot of stuff. I'm a guy, after all."

"Hey, what does that mean? You have, like, a million pairs of shoes. All brown."

"True. You don't know the half of it. Eighty percent of my clothes are not even here." He picked up the box. "I'm putting some of this stuff in my room upstairs. I'm moving back up there the day before your parents come."

"Sounds good."

"Should I give them a gift?"

"A Christmas gift?"

"No, I mean a gift for... I don't know."

"Marrying their daughter?"

"More like a welcome home present."

Clémence smiled. "You can do whatever you want. I think it's sweet of you. Maybe your mom should give me a present for taking you off her hands."

"I'm sure you'll be getting plenty of presents from her from now on."

"The pressure is on, but I like to think of myself as a pretty advanced gift giver, so you Duboirs better watch out."

"I just get my assistant to do that stuff," Arthur said.

Clémence gave him a look.

"I'm kidding!" Arthur laughed. "I don't even have an assistant. I'll buy your dad some diamond cufflinks if that makes him happy."

"Oh, you know my dad and diamonds," Clémence joked.

"I've always liked your dad. He knows a lot about my field. We've had some good conversations." Arthur worked in finance. He had recently finished his master's and had a decent job. In the past year, he'd really grown up. He'd even found an apartment for them to move into after they were married.

"And I've always liked your mom," Clémence said.

"Let's eat. I want to hear about your crazy day."

"All right, but don't say I didn't warn you."

Chapter 5

"Another murder?" Berenice exclaimed.

"Yup." Clémence nodded. She was working in Damour's massive kitchen, alongside Berenice and her brother Sebastien. Both of them were bakers. Sebastien was putting the finishing touches on an intricate chocolate cake commissioned for a special charity event. Berenice was piping the éclair fillings.

After Clémence told them about the wedding shop and Adine's assistant finding the dead body, she mentioned another unfortunate fact. "Get this. Before she died, Adine had been drinking our hot chocolate. At least, that's what Cyril said. She owned a jar of our hot chocolate mix."

"So?" Sebastien asked. "It's not like the hot chocolate was poisoned, right?"

"No, it wasn't, but do you think our products are cursed? It's kind of weird that they're found at every murder scene, isn't it?"

"We've been through this before, Clémence," Berenice said. "Everybody in Paris has something from Damour. Our stuff is not cursed. They're just so good that everyone wants a piece of it."

"Yeah. Don't listen to Cyril," Sebastien agreed. "He's just trying to push your buttons."

"Murder happens all the time," Berenice said. "Paris is a big city... a dangerous city sometimes. Don't blame yourself or your brand."

"I try to tell myself that," Clémence lamented. "And I certainly try to tell that to Cyril, but I still can't help feeling guilty, especially when I was there trying on dresses when someone discovered the body."

"Are you going to buy the dress?" Berenice asked.

"I shouldn't, right?" She paused, thinking about the beautiful lace dress. "It's so beautiful. What a shame."

"Why not?" Sebastien said. "You think the dress is cursed now too?"

"Well... maybe."

He shook his head. "Curses aren't real. You just happened to be at the wrong place at the wrong time."

"So I *should* buy the dress?"

"Well, don't take it out of the running."

"I don't know..."

Sebastien and Berenice hadn't seen the body. How could she wear something on her big day when it reminded her of a murder?

"Are you having pre-wedding jitters?" Berenice asked.

"Not really. Just shaken up because of this incident, that's all."

"Well, you've been involved in murder investigations before. You've never had a wedding."

Clémence had to laugh. "I guess that's true. Hey, at least I don't have to solve the murder this time."

"What? They caught the killer already?"

"Close. They've arrested Adine's ex-boyfriend. Apparently, this guy was so obsessed with her that he was stalking her."

"Are they sure he's the guy?" Berenice asked.

"That's what Arthur asked me last night. I don't know, but who else could it be?"

"Surely there are other suspects," Sebastien said. "I mean, is that Cyril guy ever right?"

"No," Clémence said. "He's pretty bad. The one mystery I can't solve is how he ever got to be a top inspector. Apparently, Adine wasn't that well liked.

She worked through a slew of ex-assistants. That girl, Perrie? She's only been working for her for a month. Then there's Jennifer Moss. She's Adine's business partner and co-founder of La Belle. They're close, but they also fight a lot; at least, that's what I heard from the salesgirl."

"The business partner," Sebastien said. "Look into her. With Adine dead, she would take over the whole business."

"Yes, but Adine was the designer," Berenice said. "Who would design the dresses then?"

"When designers die," Clémence said, "other designers can be hired to take over. All the fashion labels do it—Chanel, Dior, Louis Vuitton. It's possible. If Jennifer didn't get along with Adine, the only way to get rid of her was to kill her then replace her with someone she could control. After all, I did hear that Jennifer had ambitions to open more boutiques, but Adine just wanted to keep the business the way it was."

"So, you think it's Jennifer," Berenice said.

"Well, I don't know."

"It sounds like you do."

"I've been wrong before," Clémence said.

"So has Cyril."

"I can't get involved in this stuff again."

"You know you're going to." Sebastien grinned. "You can't just stand by when Cyril may have arrested the wrong person."

"Why don't you two do the investigating?" Clémence asked. "You always sound so eager."

"We're slaving in a hot kitchen all day," Sebastien said. "You think we have time?"

"Yeah," Berenice chimed in. "With the hours you got us working?"

"Hey," Clémence said mockingly angry. "You're working your dream jobs here. Besides, I'm retired from amateur detective work."

"What, now that you're getting married, you're giving up on your career?" Berenice asked.

Clémence laughed. "It's only a career if you get paid."

"Look, it's easy," Sebastien said. "You have an excuse to go poking around in that dress shop. You're still considering the dress anyway. Just make another appointment. See if that Jennifer lady is around."

"I can do that," Clémence agreed. "But I have a better idea. I might as well find out if this Noel guy is guilty or not, once and for all."

Chapter 6

Madeleine Seydoux was late. Clémence sipped her cocktail inside the chic bar near Madeleine's workplace and looked at her watch. She sat near the back, in the corner facing the door, and alternated between looking at her watch, down at her phone, and at the door.

Madeleine was only five minutes late, so Clémence didn't know why she was so anxious. She had asked her friend to meet her because she had some questions about Noel. Clémence was taking this murder case seriously. Her friends had convinced her that Cyril might be wrong, and now, every minute felt imperative.

Madeleine was the one who had recommended La Belle for wedding dress shopping. She was also planning her wedding. Although she hadn't bought one of Adine's dresses—her dress was a custom-made Vera Wang creation—she had nothing but high praise for the small boutique.

When Clémence got engaged, Madeleine had been the first friend she'd turned to for advice. Madeleine had already done a lot of research and knew all the best dress shops in town. Clémence's wedding wasn't going to be anywhere near the scope and expense of Madeleine's wedding. Her dress was probably going to be her one big splurge.

Madeleine was well known in the fashion circles. From what she'd told Clémence about La Belle, it sounded as if she knew Adine, at least on an acquaintance level. To Clémence's surprise, Madeleine didn't work in fashion, but worked in public relations. Sometimes, she did some modeling, alongside her sister, Sophie, who was getting famous because of her acting career. Sophie was out of town for a film shoot, but between the two sisters, Clémence would surely find out more about Adine's social circle and how to penetrate it.

When Clémence realized she was tapping her toes so hard that she was disturbing the man playing a game on his phone beside her, she stopped. What was she so antsy about?

She was naturally a worrywart and very sensitive to people around her. Those traits made her a good sleuth, but they also worked her nerves. As much as she liked the thrill of solving a case, she liked it better when it was over, when everything was tied together with a big bow, and she could breathe easy and get on with her life.

A few minutes later, Madeleine breezed in, looking very much like a celebrity. She wore a belted cream coat, crocodile-print heels, and carried a tan Hermes bag. She took off her oversized sunglasses and looked around the room, her eyes adjusting to the dimness of the bar. "Clémence!" Madeleine exclaimed when she spotted her friend.

Clémence stood and greeted Madeleine with air kisses. "Thanks for meeting me."

"My pleasure. I haven't seen you in, what is it, two weeks now?"

The waiter came by and greeted Madeleine by name. She frequented the bar, so she was on a first-name basis with all the employees. "Bonjour, Xavier. I'll have my usual, please."

"Of course." Xavier smiled and left.

"What's the usual?" Clémence asked her.

"It's not on the menu. It's a special cocktail they've concocted just for me. It's pomegranate based. One day, they'll probably update the menu and name the drink after me."

"Of course they will," Clémence said. "You must be really good at public relations."

"I'm the best. If Damour wasn't tied up already with our competition, we would be amazing for your brand."

"Maybe one day."

"What are you drinking? Or what *were* you drinking? Looks like it's all gone."

"A spritz." Clémence shook the empty glass. "I was nervous, waiting for you." She told Madeleine about Adine's murder.

"Adine is dead?" Madeleine asked.

"Unfortunately, she is."

"Murdered?"

Clémence nodded.

Madeleine was silent for a moment then shook her head. The waiter placed her drink on the table, but she barely noticed. "But who would want to kill her?"

"The police have an idea, but I don't know if they have the right person."

"Naturally, you're going to help them." Madeleine clasped her hands in a pleading gesture.

"I am," Clémence said. "That's why I wanted to meet you. Did you know Adine well?"

"We were good friends."

"Really?"

"Well, you know, everyone's a good friend of mine. I saw Adine at parties, charity events, things like that. It took me a while to get to her. Her partner, Jennifer, however, is more social."

"Can you tell me more about them?"

"Adine could be a bit of a wallflower at first. The first time I saw her at a party, she had her arms crossed, and it looked like she really needed to go out for a cigarette. She was more talkative when Jennifer was beside her, though. Jennifer's cool. She speaks French with a charming British accent. She's definitely better at schmoozing. Maybe that was why they made such a good team. Adine was the artist, and Jennifer was the businessperson."

"You know, the police think Adine's ex-boyfriend probably had something to do with the murder. Noel something. Do you know anything about him?"

"Noel…" Madeleine took a sip of her drink as she racked her brain. "Oh! Noel Chevalier. Yes, I know him."

"Really?" Clémence thought about what Eva had said about Noel, that he dressed shabbily, like a homeless person.

"Yes, Noel. He was a lot like Adine. He's the moody artist type. He *is* an artist, I mean. Yes, I do remember hearing that he'd broken up with her, and he was working on a bunch of new art because of that. Breakups can really inspire an artist."

"Was he well known?"

"He's moderately successful. His parents are relatively rich, so naturally, he became a bohemian bourgeois and moved to the eleventh to live 'authentically.' He always looks like he hates the parties I see him at, and I wonder why he even comes. Maybe he just wanted to be with Adine. Adine was the cool, detached one in the relationship. He was obsessed with her like John Lennon was with Yoko. Adine probably broke up with him because he was too clingy. I know I would if I were dating a guy like that."

"Oh, wow. He was that obsessed?" Perhaps the police were right. Noel did have motive. If he'd been madly in love, and Adine had coldly rejected him, it could've been a crime of passion. "Do you think he could've killed her?"

"Noel?" Madeleine gasped. "He's a sensitive artist but not a murderer."

"Really? But I thought you said he was obsessed."

"I know guys like that. They're sweethearts. They're sensitive but not violent. Noel would brood and mope and cry. He probably even enjoys feeling his pain this deeply."

"But I heard that he had been stalking her, so much that Adine wanted to get a restraining order."

"Well, I didn't know about that, but Noel probably wouldn't hurt a fly. He'd cry and slit his own wrists before he would kill Adine with such brutality."

"The police already have him in custody," Clémence said. "They're serious about him. They really think he did it."

"*What?*"

"Apparently, he had been hanging around Adine's place earlier in the morning on the day her body was found."

"I just can't believe it," Madeleine said. "I just don't think he's the type. He's a lovelorn Romeo, sure, and maybe he was just hanging around, trying to get a glimpse of her at the window. I can't imagine he would break in and bash her in the head."

"So who would?" Clémence asked. "Is there anyone else you can think of? I heard Adine was not well liked."

"From what I could tell, she was maybe a bit frosty, but once she liked you, she was very nice."

"But everyone likes *you*," Clémence said. "You're a social butterfly, you're charming, and you're popular. Plus you have status. Apparently, Adine didn't treat the people below her very well, like her assistants, for example."

"Hmm. I wouldn't know about that."

"What do you know about Jennifer?"

"She's a very bright girl with a business background, and she's very ambitious. She has big ideas for their brand. She almost sold me on one of their dresses before I went to Vera Wang."

Clémence knew that type. *Jennifer sounds like someone who would stop at nothing to get what she wants.* The Paris fashion industry was tough. Sometimes, people were so ambitious, they became ruthless. If Noel wasn't the guy, Jennifer would be the next person Clémence wanted to check out. If she wasn't the killer, at least Clémence would have the contact information for Adine's former assistants.

"I would really like to talk to her," Clémence said. "Do you have her number?"

"I do. I'll forward it to you right now."

"When was the last time you saw or talked to her?"

"It must be at least a month ago, at Marcus's birthday party."

"Oh, they were there too?" Clémence asked. Marcus was a friend of hers. He was a well-known fashion designer who threw extravagant parties.

"Everybody was there. It was a zoo."

"Yeah, no wonder I didn't see them."

After they finished their drinks, Clémence called Jennifer, but it went straight to voicemail. She left a message, saying she was Madeleine's friend and that she urgently wanted to talk to her.

She wondered where Jennifer was. Perhaps she was at the boutique. But it was close to dinnertime, and the shop was definitely closed. Clémence would have to check another time.

Chapter 7

As soon as Clémence stepped into her apartment, she smelled the delicious aroma. She was hungrier than she'd thought, and the cocktails she'd had with Madeleine had made her lightheaded.

"I made chicken," Arthur said from the kitchen.

"You did?" Clémence greeted him with a hug and a kiss on the cheek.

Arthur was classically handsome, with chestnut brown hair and eyes to match. He'd grown up rather spoiled. His family employed two cooks, so he didn't know anything about being in a kitchen. His nannies and maids pampered him. He'd only recently learned to do things himself, like cleaning and cooking. Clémence was glad he didn't expect her to do all the work in their household, and that he was making some domestic efforts. If that was a sign of things to come in their marriage, she welcomed it.

With oven gloves on, he took the tray out of the oven. "What do you think?"

"It certainly smells like chicken," Clémence said. "How did you make it?"

"It turned out not to be that difficult. I asked Andre for advice, and he gave me a list of spices to put on the chicken."

"That's great," she exclaimed. "Who's Andre?"

"Our chef. Well, he's new. Our old chef retired."

"I see. Tell Andre I thank him for my dinner."

"What about me?"

"Oh, right," she teased. "Thank you for the chicken."

"I also cooked green beans." He pointed to a pot on the stove. "It must've been great to have grown up with parents who cooked."

"Sometimes they cooked on the weekends, but honestly, they were pretty busy most of the time, so they just had our chefs whip up things from Damour, or we ate leftovers."

"That sounds even better," Arthur said. "Plus you must've eaten so many desserts. Our mother didn't let us have a lot of sugar. We would salivate in front of patisseries and candy stores."

Clémence laughed. "It's not as if they let me wolf down five chocolate croissants a day. I got to have a small treat after school, but that was about it. Sugar and little kids don't mix."

"Tell me about it. My younger brothers used to climb chairs to get to the snacks in the top cupboards. By the time the nanny found them, they were running around like crazy with chocolate-stained cheeks."

Clémence helped set up the plates and utensils on the table. Arthur uncorked the wine. Miffy barked, wanting attention. Clémence kneeled and gave her head a good rub.

"Are you hungry?" Arthur asked.

"I'm always hungry. You've been doing a lot of cooking lately. Thinking about becoming a chef?"

"You know what? I like it. It's a de-stresser after a long day at work. I'm starting with simple dishes. Maybe one day, I'll learn how to make a proper three-course meal."

"I'm not a picky eater." Clémence smiled. "Those skills will come in handy when we throw dinner parties."

"That's what married people do, right? Throw dinner parties?"

"At least that's what my parents did. I have to say my favorite dinner party was in America. My uncle—my mother's little brother—and his wife used to have make-your-own pizza parties. They had a stone oven in their backyard. Guests would come over and make their own pizzas with the variety of toppings available, and they would compete to see who created the best-tasting one."

"Why did you have to bring up pizza?" Arthur said. "Now I'm craving pizza."

He dished up a chicken leg for Clémence, knowing it was her favorite piece of the chicken.

"This is delicious, though," Clémence said after a bite. "You'll forget all about pizza after you taste this."

After Arthur distributed the green beans and put some salt and pepper on his food, he tried it. "It's not half bad. It's almost as good as Andre's."

"Almost?"

"The chicken is not as tender for some reason. I don't know if it's me or the chicken. I'll have to ask him."

"The chicken is great. I'm not kidding. Restaurant quality."

After another few bites, he agreed. "You're right. I've had some chicken in restaurants that was absolutely rubbery. This is a lot better."

"Look at you, Chef Duboir."

"It makes sense. You being the baker, and me the chef. It's a gastronomic match made in heaven." When Arthur smiled, a dimple appeared in his left cheek. It made him look sweet, like a little boy. Just a year ago, "sweet" would've been the last word Clémence would have used to describe him.

After they ate their meals, they finished the bottle of wine, which was something they did more often than not. Arthur talked about his day at work, then they discussed world events and politics before Clémence brought up her news about the murder case.

"So, Noel, you know, Adine's ex-boyfriend who was arrested? Well, there's a chance he might be innocent."

"I knew it," Arthur said. "The Paris police always screw it up."

"I wouldn't say that they screwed it up yet—"

"But you're going to investigate, right?"

She nodded. "It might be Jennifer Moss, Adine's longtime business partner, but she's nowhere to be found. Madeleine sort of knows her. She gave me her number, and I left her a message, but she hasn't returned my call. I called that girl Perrie, Adine's assistant, and she said she hasn't seen or heard from Jennifer since Adine died."

"You said Jennifer's British, right? I wonder if she was even in town when the murder happened."

"That's what I'm trying to find out. Or what if she committed the murder then fled the country?"

"You're not going to rest until you find out, are you?"

"You know me too well," Clémence said.

"Go for it. Let me know if you need any help. We have a cake tasting tomorrow afternoon, but I'll reschedule it to next week."

"Why next week?"

"According to my calculations—and I am very much a finance guy, as you know—you'll solve this by early next week."

"Are you kidding? That's only a few days!"

"It doesn't usually take you more than two weeks to solve a case. I expect you to have it wrapped up before the cake tasting. In the meantime, I don't expect you to do any work at Damour or come home on time for dinner."

"I hope that's okay."

"When has it not been? I trust you to solve the case soon, anyway."

"Don't say that, or you'll jinx me."

Chapter 8

*E*arly in the morning, Clémence kissed Arthur good-bye after breakfast. He left for work, and she took Miffy for a walk in Champs de Mars, the park under the Eiffel Tower. She wanted to clear her head before the day started, and the weather was lovely. The gray winter clouds had dispersed, and the sun had finally come out after weeks of playing peekaboo.

As usual, tourists were posing in front of the Eiffel Tower, doing funny poses, like pretending to push the Tower. It was cheesy, but Clémence still liked tourists in Paris. They reminded her that she lived in a city that made other people happy, and she felt lucky to live there. On days when she had bad traffic, dreary weather, crowded metros, or murders to think about, she enjoyed reminders that Paris was as beautiful as everyone said.

Even though Clémence wasn't sure whether she would end up buying a wedding dress from a murdered designer, she took out her cell phone and made another appointment for later that day. The saleswoman named Laurie had answered. Clémence had been afraid La Belle would remain closed, but Laurie assured her they were still taking appointments. The next one available with Eva was that afternoon.

"Did the other owner agree to keep the store open?" Clémence asked.

"Oh, Jennifer?" Laurie asked. "Actually, I haven't spoken to her. Sometimes, she does that. She goes out of town. When she's away, I manage the store."

"I see. And you haven't seen or heard from her either?"

"No. I tried leaving messages on her phone. I guess we'll hear from her when we hear from her."

"Any idea where she might be?"

"I have no idea. I'm sorry."

"Okay. See you at three thirty, then."

"Great! Thanks for calling."

As Miffy sniffed around the bushes, Clémence texted Celine, asking if she could come with her to the boutique after her shift. She knew Celine was working the morning shift and would get off around three o'clock that afternoon.

Oui! Celine texted back. *Can't wait.*

After Miffy became tired from running around, Clémence brought her back to the apartment. The sun had returned to its blanket of clouds, and Clémence tossed an umbrella in her handbag just in case it rained.

The flagship family patisserie was at 2 Place du Trocadéro. When the weather was nicer, they opened up the front as an outdoor patio. The store had a stunning view of the Eiffel Tower, and tourists and locals alike frequented their place.

When Clémence arrived, the line for the patisserie section was out the door. The cashiers were working as fast as they could. They were used to the morning rush of customers wanting to grab a fresh croissant or treat before the morning started. The shop also sold espressos for the caffeine addicts. However, the patisserie didn't have seats, so the customers usually took their shots at the counter and grabbed their treats to go.

Customers could sit in the *salon de thé* section of the establishment. They could have a cup of tea or eat a full meal there. In recent years, business was doing so well that customers couldn't stop in and grab a seat anymore. Tables had to be booked in advance. Sometimes, Clémence missed the good old days when older customers would read their newspapers at a leisurely pace, or students would drop in after work and do their homework. They still had customers like that from time to time, during seasons when it wasn't so busy.

Celine was the first person she saw when she entered the *salon de thé*. Dressed in her classy uniform of black pants and a crisp white dress shirt, Celine greeted her with air kisses. "I can't wait to go to that shop later. Sorry I missed your last appointment."

"You shouldn't be. You missed seeing a dead body."

"That's true. I was just really hoping to help you find a dress. Are you really going there for that dress or to investigate?"

"A little bit of both, I suppose," Clémence admitted. "I do really, really like the dress, and I need a second opinion. You don't think it's weird, do you?"

"No. It might be a good way of honoring the designer."

"I didn't think of it that way. Maybe you're right. The police think they have it figured out, but I still think it's odd that Jennifer hasn't been in the shop. I wonder if the police have clued into that yet."

"So, she's just missing?"

"Yup. It's odd. The salesperson doesn't think it's unusual, though. Jennifer's British, so she might've been out of the country. Being a founder of the store doesn't require her to be in the store all the time. Still, I think it's odd that she didn't call me back. You'd think someone who travels back and forth would have a phone plan that takes calls from France in the UK."

"Did her phone ring, or did it go straight to voicemail?"

"It rang." Clémence took out her cell phone from her purse. "You know what? I'll call her again." She made the call, and it went straight to voicemail. "Nope, no ringing this time."

"That's odd," Celine remarked.

Clémence shrugged. "We'll try to figure it out at the boutique, ask some more questions, see if there's anything suspicious going on."

Customers came in, and Celine had to attend to them.

"We'll strategize at lunchtime," Clémence said.

"Sure. I can't believe I get to work on a murder case with you."

Luckily, Celine only whispered the last part.

As usual, when Clémence worked on a case, she couldn't concentrate on her real job in the kitchen. Usually, she experimented with new flavors of macarons, éclairs, and other baked goods, helping Sebastien and Berenice with their inventions or custom orders, but when her brain was occupied, she was more of a passive baker. She went into machine-mode, where her body worked, and her brain tumbled with thoughts and theories.

She helped make holiday gingerbread cookies, which were American. Since her mother was American, Damour never shied away from infusing foreign treats and recipes with homegrown ones.

By lunchtime, Clémence had managed to make and package a few holiday cookie boxes. She'd kept busy with the repetitive work of baking, decorating, and packaging, but her mind wandered to the crime.

Noel was still a suspect, even if Madeleine thought otherwise. He had enough motive, and he was even spotted at the scene of the crime. Adine had also known him. There was no sign of a break-in. Although Adine may have felt compelled to file a restraining order against him, perhaps he had convinced her to let him in.

Jennifer was missing, and even her employees had not heard from her. That seemed highly unusual for a business owner. With phones, email, and social media, Jennifer could have easily checked in on the store, and she could have heard through friends and employees that Adine was dead. Then again, just because Clémence and the employees hadn't heard from Jennifer, she could have gone directly to the police or Adine's family and had been in too much of a shock to check in with anyone else.

Perhaps Clémence should check with Cyril about that. He may have thought she was a drag, but when she showed up at his office, she usually left with information.

There were also Adine's assistants to look into.

"Do you think Perrie could have done it?" Celine asked during a quick lunch break.

Clémence had written all the suspects and their motives down in her notebook. "I doubt it."

"How do you know?" Celine asked between spoonfuls of her homemade red quinoa with spinach and mushrooms. "How long has she been working for Adine?"

"Not long. A month, maybe. I just don't think she did it. It's just an instinct."

"Who knows? Maybe you should look into her history."

"I suppose I can ask Eva, the saleswoman I'm meeting, later today."

"Eva. How about her? Could she have done it?"

Clémence thought about it. "I didn't consider her. I mean, she was working in the boutique."

"She has access to the atelier, doesn't she?"

"I suppose, but she was working. Who kills an employer in the middle of a shift? And why?"

Celine shrugged. "I don't know. I'm just looking at all possible angles."

"Okay." Clémence wrote it down, using a new page for each suspect. It didn't hurt to look into it. She hadn't considered Eva. For her to have killed Adine would have been unlikely. "Eva has known Jennifer and Adine for five years. She told me."

"So there's history there."

"I suppose."

"And who's to say that just because Perrie has been working for Adine for one month, she didn't have history with her before that? What if she weaseled her way into a job just to kill her then pretend to be innocent upon finding her?"

Clémence shook her head. "I really don't know about these two suspects, but I'll keep an open mind. I do want to know more about these former assistants. Maybe I'll look into that."

"Just remember," Celine said in a grave voice. "Everyone you talk to might be a murderer."

"Wow." Clémence laughed. "I'll try not to forget that."

"Was that too dramatic?" Celine asked. "I was trying to sound like someone in one of those murder dramas."

"Well, you've succeeded. So, let's see. This afternoon, we shall go find a wedding dress and then a murderer."

"Sounds easy enough," Celine said.

Chapter 9

*A*fter lunch, Clémence took over Berenice's task of piping a few trays of éclairs with chocolate. The work was meditative, killing her impatience and anxiousness to get to the bottom of the case. When three o'clock came, she went with Celine to the 6th arrondissement.

Celine had changed out of her uniform into jeans, boots, and a gray coat. It was chilly outside, and Clémence wrapped a big wool scarf around herself in two loops. She smelled like sweet pastries. She always did when she got out of the kitchen. Arthur liked it, and he told her he had come to associate the smell of patisseries with Clémence.

The girls jumped into the Métro, which was the fastest way to the store with all the afternoon traffic. Hordes of tourists had descended on Paris for the holiday season, which was an even busier time than the summer.

Christmas was Clémence's favorite holiday. Even though it was more celebrated in other parts of the world, like America, the lights and décor in Paris weren't too shabby. On Champs-Élysée, the lights were already up, and she couldn't wait to see what the window displays at Galeries Lafayette were going to look like. They were usually extravagant spectacles, and tourists would crowd before them, making them almost impossible to see.

At least she had beaten the holiday rush by buying half of her presents online. She'd bought a new stationery kit for her mother, with her initials on the box and on the letterheads; a beard and moustache kit for her father, complete with organic beard oil and a little brush; a trendy jacket for her sister; and an antique pocket watch for her brother. She knew her family well. She would have to poke around the shops in Paris to buy her remaining presents, but at least her immediate family was covered.

As for Arthur, she was still searching. What could she get the man who had everything? He certainly had enough brown brogues.

"You're so lucky to be getting married," Celine said on the Métro.

A subway performer was playing the accordion, and Clémence couldn't hear Celine very well, so she asked her to repeat herself.

"I said you're so lucky to be getting married!" Celine repeated loudly.

"Yes," Clémence said. "Thanks. You'll get married someday too, don't forget."

"It seems like an impossibility right now."

Celine was one of Clémence's few friends who were single at the moment. Clémence could understand how she felt. She'd had times in her life in which she'd felt as though everyone was coupled off except her. Her siblings both married young, and after she'd broken up with her cheating boyfriend, she'd traveled the world to find herself. When she'd returned and was in a better place, she'd found love when she'd least expected to.

"You just can't predict these kinds of things," Clémence said. "Last year, I was so single, I felt like I was going to be alone forever. I didn't even want love. I hated being cheated on. Even though I tried to date, I wasn't open. Well, you know my story. Things just happen, and the universe orchestrates events that you can't control."

"That's the problem," Celine said. "I'm impatient. It feels like I've been waiting forever... like every-where I go, I'm met with dead ends."

"Don't worry. You won't get stuck in the maze. Just think of every wrong guy you date as a bread crumb to the right guy."

"Have you seen the guys I've dated? There was at least one murderer!"

Clémence chuckled. "You live and you learn, right? What's the rush, anyway? You want to have children?"

"I don't know. It's not something I think about."

"Then keep busy and happy. Be happy for everyone who has love too. It's not easy to find."

"It's kind of like a miracle," Celine agreed. "How do people find each other? I just feel like I'm left out sometimes, and I hate that."

"Oh, Celine." Clémence gave her a hug. "You won't feel left out. Ever. We're still your family. You know that. We're all rooting for you."

"Thanks." Celine smiled.

"Are you dating anyone now?"

"I went out for a drink with someone last week. He's doing his PhD in philosophy."

"Sounds impressive."

"I tried to give him a chance, but philosophy is so boring. Plus his breath stank."

Clémence laughed. "Okay, that's a deal breaker. At least you're getting out there. You're doing everything you can. You'll meet him one day."

"I hope so."

At street level, Clémence led the way to La Belle. Once they passed the busy shopping streets and stepped into the intimate cobblestone alleys, they reached La Belle's beautiful window display of elegant white dresses.

"Oh, they're all so pretty," Celine said. "I love everything I see already."

"Brace yourself," Clémence warned. She pushed the door open. "Hello?"

A slim woman with long black hair walked toward them from the back of the store. "Hi, you must be Clémence."

"Laurie?"

"Yes, I spoke to you on the phone today."

Clémence nodded and smiled. "I made an appointment to see Eva. Is she here?"

"Unfortunately, she's not. I'm sorry. However, I'm available to help you."

"Oh." Clémence was clearly disappointed. "What happened to Eva?"

"She's not feeling well today. She asked me to take over and help you. I hope that's okay."

"Of course. This is my friend Celine. She's going to help me with my decision today."

"Nice to meet you, Celine."

"I hope Eva's okay," Clémence said.

"I think yesterday took a toll on her," Laurie replied. "The murder of our boss, and then all that police interrogation. I was out of town, so I didn't know about it until the evening when Eva called me." She shook her head. "I can't believe something like that could happen here."

"It's sad," Celine agreed.

"Eva's been here for years, so it must be so hard on her," Laurie said.

"How long have you been here?"

"About seven months. I used to live and work in a department store in the south of France, so this is my first job in Paris. I moved here to be with my boyfriend. With recent events, though, I've been trying to convince him to move down south with me. Not only is it less dangerous, but the weather is less depressing, and the people are more relaxed." She shook her head, coming out of her reverie. "Anyway, let's get started. I pulled out the dress you wanted to see again, according to Eva's instructions."

"So, it's only you and Eva working here?" Clémence asked.

Laurie nodded. "Sometimes our shifts overlap. There's not really room for more than two sales-people anyway. Plus, we usually take one appointment at a time. Two, if we know that the bride-to-be won't be bringing a lot of people. Sometimes, they bring a whole entourage. Once, this woman brought twelve people. They all barely fit inside the shop!" She shook her head, tut-tutting. "I do hope this store won't close down because of the awful murder. It's such a lovely shop, with dresses more beautiful than the big brands, but who knows? With the designer gone, I don't know what they're going to do. I didn't see anything in the papers today about Adine, but I'm sure clients will start hearing about it soon."

"Where's Jennifer?"

"I haven't seen or heard from her."

"That's a bit strange, don't you think?" Celine said.

"Jennifer? She's often away in London."

"Yes, but shouldn't she be easy to get in contact with? Shouldn't she know that Adine is dead?"

"Oh, she'll find out eventually. I mean, sometimes Jennifer just gets busy. La Belle is not her priority anymore." Laurie gave them a strange look. "Do you mean to suggest she could be the murderer? The police already arrested Noel."

"Well..." Clémence said slowly. "What if it wasn't Noel? And what exactly do you mean that La Belle is not her priority anymore?"

"I hear Jennifer used to be more invested in La Belle. She wanted to expand the boutiques. I used to hear them arguing about it in the atelier. Adine didn't want to expand, and after a while, Jennifer just gave up. She started spending more time outside of the store. I assumed since Adine wasn't agreeing to her plans, she was working on other projects. I heard she did some business consulting on the side, but I don't know for sure. I never asked her about it, because it's none of my business."

"How's the store doing financially?" Clémence asked.

"Between you and me? More than well. This is the best-paying job I've had. Adine could have been a big designer, but she refused to expand for some reason. She was so talented." Laurie took the dress off the rack. "Here. Are you ready to try it on?"

Clémence had more questions to ask, but she figured she could use a break. When she came out in the lace dress, Celine swooned. "I see what you mean now. It's very you, but not you at the same time. It's bold yet classy."

"So, do you think I should wear this on my wedding day?"

"I haven't seen any others, but this is nice." Celine turned to Laurie. "Can we see her jacked up with the veil and everything?"

"Of course. I'll be right back."

"It really hugs your curves," Celine said to Clémence. Tears formed in her eyes.

"You're crying?" Clémence asked.

"It's just so beautiful, and I can picture you walking down the aisle already. I'm so proud to be one of your bridesmaids."

"And you'll look lovely in your dress too."

"You are the best bride, letting us wear whatever dress we want. Aren't you afraid they're all going to clash?"

"No. It'll be great to have some eccentricity. I'm sure whatever you wear will be lovely."

Laurie came back with two options for veils.

"I think these two would work quite nicely." She held up one in each hand.

The two veils were almost identical in Clémence's eyes, so she chose one at random. She turned around, and Laurie helped put it on her. When Clémence turned back to the mirror, she thought she looked like a real bride. All she needed was a bouquet of flowers.

"You look like a movie star from the '30s," Celine said. "A movie star getting married. I can't imagine you finding a dress more beautiful."

"I'm afraid you might be right," Clémence said, sighing.

"You don't sound happy about that," Laurie noted.

"The thing is," Clémence started, "Adine was murdered. Would it be bad luck to wear this?"

"I know it's a difficult time," Celine said. "But there have been designers who were murdered. Like Gianni Versace. Do we stop wearing his clothes? It's not his fault someone killed him."

"Look at it this way," Laurie said. "I'm sure wherever Adine is, she would be flattered that you chose her design."

Clémence looked at herself in the mirror, turning around in a circle. "Let me think about it. The wedding is still seven months away. I have some time to decide." The truth was, she didn't feel comfortable buying the dress until the murder case was resolved. "Is Perrie around?"

"Perrie's not working today. Actually, I don't even know if she still works here since she worked for Adine."

"I'd like to talk to her," Clémence said. "I didn't get a chance to get her number. Do you mind if we contact her?"

"What did you want to talk to her about?" Laurie asked.

"What else?" Celine said. "The murder."

Chapter 10

*A*fter Clémence insinuated she worked for the police, she easily convinced Laurie to give them Perrie's number. Clémence called her as soon as she and Celine left the boutique.

As Laurie had feared, Perrie wasn't sure if she had a job anymore. "I tried to get in touch with Jennifer," Perrie said on the phone, "but she's not answering my calls or emails, and she hasn't been on Facebook or Skype. I have no idea where she is."

"Have you tried calling anyone she knows?"

"Yes. I have her parents' home number. They live in a suburb of London. I thought Jennifer might be there, but they said she was in London two weeks ago. She's supposed to be in Paris, as far as they know."

"This is weird," Clémence said. "Have you tried going to her home?"

"No. Should we?" Perrie paused. "What if she is the killer? This is getting too weird. She's supposed to be in town, but she hides from everyone?"

"Okay, we'll get to the bottom of this. Do you have her address?"

"Yes."

"Text it to me," Clémence said.

"I can do that. I don't actually live far from Jennifer's apartment, so I'm nearby. I'm in the café a block away. They have Internet here. I've actually been looking for a new job all day."

"Text me the address of the café too. We'll meet you there, then we'll go together."

"It's about three blocks from La Belle. I'll text you right now."

Clémence and Celine only needed to walk five minutes until they reached Le Café Vert, a modern café located in the 6th arrondissement and bordering the 5th.

"I really don't think Perrie is a suspect," Clémence said. "I'll keep my ears open if she lets anything slip, but right now, my money's on Jennifer."

"The whole thing is really odd," Celine agreed. "It gives me the creeps. Should we call the police?"

"I'm tempted to, but it wouldn't hurt to knock on the door at least and see what she says before we jump to any conclusions."

"What if she's dangerous?"

"There's three of us," Clémence said. "Plus, I learned some basic self-defense moves."

"I guess you've been in enough dangerous situations to know what you're talking about," Celine said.

Perrie was deep inside the bright cafe, tapping away on a MacBook. An empty cappuccino cup and a newspaper were on her table. When Clémence and Celine walked up, Perrie stood up and practically hugged Clémence, even though that was not the French custom. "I'm so relieved to see you. To tell you the truth, I don't have a lot of friends in Paris, and the events in the last couple of days have really freaked me out."

"This is my friend Celine," Clémence said.

"Nice to meet you," Celine said.

"Hi. Sit down, please." Perrie gestured to the seats around her table.

"How did you start working for Adine, anyway?" Clémence asked.

"I actually went to Italy to study fashion," Perrie explained. "My mother is Italian. My parents are divorced, and my father lives in Strasbourg. Anyway,

I was just applying for jobs everywhere. I went on a bunch of interviews in Paris, and I got the job. It wasn't very well paying, but it was something. I couldn't get anything in Italy." She sighed. "A month in, and I find my boss's head bashed in. It's shocking that something like this could happen. I'm still numbed by it."

"What was it like to work for her?" Celine asked.

"This was my first real job working for a fashion designer. Friends warned me that it would be grueling. Since it was a small boutique, I didn't expect it to be that bad, but it turned out to be challenging, that's for sure."

"Because of Adine, or because of the work involved?"

"Both. I was always running around or working long hours. I did everything from fetching coffee to booking venues for runway shows. Well, at least that was what I would be doing if I'd kept working long enough. Since I'd only been working at La Belle for a month, I only did the grunt work. No complaints there. A job in fashion is a job. It would go on my résumé, and I'm grateful."

"Did you know about the other assistants that have left before you?"

"Not really," Perrie said.

"Nobody told you? Not even Eva?"

"No. Why? What did she say about the other assistants?"

"Just that they never lasted long," Clémence said. "That they quit and harbored hard feelings toward Adine for being so demanding."

"Honestly, Adine could be demanding, but she wasn't so vicious to me. I understood she could be moody or frustrated when she was designing, but she never personally berated me. When she was in a mood, she went up to her room, or she just muttered to herself. I kept out of her way."

"So you didn't find her tough to work for?"

"The thing with Adine was that she was really hard on herself. She strived for excellence. Sometimes, she would complain if I got her a latte that wasn't hot enough, or frivolous things like that, but I didn't take those things that personally. Those insults weren't directed at me. She just needed to blow off a little steam. I have a thick skin. I mean, my fashion program was very competitive. Girls were way meaner."

"Did you know that Jennifer wanted to open up more boutiques?" Clémence asked.

"No, I didn't know that."

"I wonder if that was why Adine didn't want to expand. She didn't feel like her designs were good enough because she was such a perfectionist."

"That could be it," Perrie said. "If she was deep in designing, I tried to make as little noise as possible. I don't know why she would worry, though. They usually came out beautifully in the end."

"Yes. Jennifer was adamant about expanding, but she gave up. Do you know if she's working somewhere else on the side?"

"Yeah," Perrie said. "She manages the boutique part-time, but Eva does a lot of the work, so Jennifer doesn't have a lot to do. I think she's a freelance business consultant on the side, so she works with different companies—startups and things like that. I only know about that because Adine was venting to me once about it. She wanted Jennifer to be more committed to La Belle, which is confusing if Jennifer did want to be more involved and expand La Belle and Adine refused to expand."

"Something weird is going on," Celine said. "That's for sure. The two women didn't agree on a lot. Now, one is dead, and the other is missing."

"I hope it's nothing horrible." Perrie furrowed her brows. "One dead boss is all I can take. Jennifer is really nice, even if I don't see her that much. She's smart, and she likes to keep busy. That's why she's always on the go."

"What do you say we go stop by her home now?" Clémence asked.

"Sure." Perrie took out some keys from her bag. "I actually have the key to her place."

"Really?" Celine asked. Clémence thought she could hear a note of suspicion in her friend's voice. "How did you get it?"

"This is actually Adine's spare key to Jennifer's place. She gave it to me last week because I needed to get some papers from Jennifer's apartment, but Jennifer wasn't around. I had it in my bag and forgot to give it back to Adine."

"If she's not there, this could be useful." Clémence stood, prompting Perrie and Celine to get moving with her. "Let's see what Jennifer has been up to."

Chapter 11

Jennifer lived above a luxury shoe store that Clémence was no stranger to.

Perrie had the six-digit code to the small blue door beside it. "I've only been here once. She's on the third floor. Her place is surprisingly big. I wish I could afford an apartment like that. Instead, I'm stuck living in a *chambre de bonne*."

Chambres de bonne were tiny rooms on the top floors of many apartment buildings in Paris. Maids used to live in them in the olden days. Arthur technically lived in a chambre de bonne in their building to maintain his independence, but at least he had access to his family's main apartment.

On the third floor, there were only two doors. Perrie turned to the one on the right and knocked.

No one answered. "Jennifer?" Perrie knocked again. "Jennifer. It's me, Perrie."

Clémence and Celine looked at each other. Perrie gave up knocking after a while. "Looks like she's not in."

Clémence gave Jennifer a call one last time. "Her phone is definitely off."

"What if she's kidnapped?" Celine asked.

"Kidnapped?" Perrie looked concerned.

"Yeah, what if she didn't flee or disappear, but she got kidnapped?"

"If we see something in her home, we'll notify the police," Clémence said. "We should probably be reporting her as a missing person at this point too. If her parents haven't heard from her either, this is serious."

Perrie put in the key and unlocked the door. Before she could push the door open, she stopped and stepped back. "I'm getting flashbacks to the scene with Adine. You go. Make sure there's no dead body in there." She gave a nervous laugh.

Clémence didn't respond. She opened the door slowly. "Jennifer?"

Silence.

Gingerly, Clémence stepped in. The living room was clear, other than a stack of magazines on the coffee table. The blinds were down, half-open, letting in some light.

"Anybody in here?" When Clémence turned toward the kitchen, she saw her. A blonde lying face down. A small pool of blood had formed around her face. It wasn't as gruesome and bloody as Adine's crime scene, but still disturbing nonetheless. She turned back to Perrie and Celine at the door. "I think it's time to call the police."

"What did you touch?" Cyril demanded.

"Nothing," Clémence said. "I just stepped inside, looked around, and saw her there. She must've been killed in the last twenty-four hours, right?"

Cyril didn't confirm it. He only asked, "Did you touch her body?"

"No. I'm not going to put my DNA all over a dead body. Are you nuts?"

"What about your friends?"

"They stayed outside."

Cyril narrowed his eyes at her, but he nodded. "Good."

"All I touched was the door and the doorknob. I don't think that matters, however. The door doesn't look to be tampered with. Either Jennifer let the killer in, or the killer had the key."

"You had the key," Cyril said. "Did you not?"

"Yes. Well, it was Adine's key. She gave it to Perrie."

Cyril gave Perrie, who was being questioned by his colleague, a long, hard look. "Perrie was the one who found Adine. Now she has the key to Jennifer's apartment, and Jennifer happens to be dead. I'm not suggesting she's the murderer..."

"Really?" Clémence said. "That sounds exactly like what you're doing. What about Noel? He's innocent now?"

"The case against Noel is strong. He wouldn't confess, but we still have him. What if he was in cahoots with Perrie? How much do you know about her anyway?"

"She's just a girl who wants to work in fashion," Clémence said. "She barely just graduated from school. She's not a killer."

"Fashion is a dangerous industry, as you should know by now. These people will stop at nothing to succeed."

"What would Perrie get out of killing her employers? Seems strange."

"Noel comes from a wealthy family," Cyril said. "What if he bribed her? After all, she's probably working for minimum wage."

Clémence did recall Perrie saying she would like a bigger apartment. She shook her head to break that line of thinking. "No, this is nuts. If this murder was committed while Noel was in custody, that means there's another killer out there. If you fixate on him or Perrie, you're not covering all your bases. Why would Noel want to kill Jennifer if he was only obsessed with Adine?"

"Maybe Jennifer was a witness."

"And what, he hired Perrie to do the dirty work for him?"

"She looks sweet." Cyril was still analyzing the girl. "Sometimes, it's the people you least suspect."

Chapter 12

Celine left the scene of the crime with more questions than answers.

"Cyril is crazy," Clémence said. "Isn't he? Noel couldn't have hired Perrie to kill Jennifer."

"It is a bit far-fetched," Celine admitted. "What if Noel *was* still the culprit for killing Adine, and coincidentally, someone else killed Jennifer around the same time."

"A coincidence? No, I don't think so. Both women were bashed in the head. They fell face down, which meant they didn't see the attack coming. This was someone they both knew."

"Perrie," Celine said. "I know she's sweet, with those innocent Bambi eyes, but what if she was involved?"

"I went over that with Cyril, but it doesn't make sense. What would Perrie gain from killing Adine and Jennifer? If she's really who she says she is, she's out of a job. However, I doubt she'd be poor enough to be out on the street. I'm sure her parents would take her in if she really couldn't find a job. That girl has no motivation to kill."

"She could always be a hostess," Celine said. "There's always room for people in the service industry."

Clémence turned to her. "You like your job, don't you, Celine?"

"At Damour? Of course. I see my favorite people every day. Why?"

"Just wanted to make sure. I know you've been working there for years. If you're ever bored and want to do something else, I didn't want you to feel obligated."

"I consider it a privilege to work at Damour. A lot of friends complain about the long work hours at their office jobs. I rather prefer the service industry. It's fun. I get to talk to people, see my friends. I never went to college. That just wasn't the path for me. I don't need a lot. I like my apartment, and a simple life is good enough for me."

"So you see yourself working at Damour for a long time, then?"

"Perhaps," Celine said. "One day, I might open up a bar, but who knows? I want a job where I can talk to people, not be stuck behind a desk from nine to five."

"Good." Clémence smiled. Sometimes, she worried about her friend, but she had to open her mind and realize some people really didn't place happiness on status and money. Even though she had studied art, the students there were egotistical and competitive. They'd bragged about being famous one day. She would rather have a friend like Celine, who had a humble job and liked it, than an overachieving one who thought what they did was who they were.

One guy Celine had dated, who was in Clémence's social circle, had been an heir to his father's publishing company. His family had looked down on Celine once they'd found out she was a hostess. However, that guy turned out to be a murderer, so it wasn't Celine's loss. Sometimes she felt overprotective of Celine.

"Anyway, I just don't know about any of this," Clémence said. "Noel and Perrie, either on their own or working together—I just don't think it's a possibility."

"So back to the drawing board?"

Clémence nodded. "Yup. The few employees working at La Belle have nothing to gain from their employers' murders. I'd have to look into those former assistants."

"It wouldn't hurt," Celine agreed.

"Noel!" Clémence exclaimed.

"What?"

"Cyril said that he's out of police custody, so he should be available to talk."

"Right now?"

"I don't know about right now," Clémence said. "I don't know where he is."

"It's been a long day, Clémence. Why don't we both go home and get some rest? Noel is probably too exhausted to talk anyway."

"You're probably right. It'll be better to talk to him tomorrow. But you're working tomorrow, right?"

"I am," Celine said. "All day too. I'm covering for Marianne for a few hours. She's got a dentist appointment."

"The dentist." Clémence shuddered. A crazy dentist had tried to kill her once, and she was put off by dentists more than ever.

"It was interesting investigating with you, though," Celine said. "Hope you solve this thing soon."

"I'll try. Too bad you can't come. I liked having you as a partner. Hope you had fun."

"I don't know about fun. I'm not sure that I'm used to dead bodies yet."

"Fun is the wrong word, huh?"

"I'll probably have nightmares tonight."

After eating dinner with Arthur, Clémence looked out of her kitchen window and saw that Berenice was visiting Ben. The two of them were standing and talking at Ben's window.

Clémence tried waving to catch their attention, but they didn't turn to look down at her.

Ben lived in one of the chambres de bonne on the top floor, down the hall from Arthur's room. Sometimes, when they were both looking out the window, they would wave at each other. Ben often dropped by to have a drink and a chat with Clémence and Arthur.

Since Berenice was over, Clémence thought it would be nice for them to come over and share the rest of the wine she and Arthur had opened at dinner.

Not long after Clémence sent Ben a text, they came down the stairs and knocked on the kitchen door.

After dating Ben for months, Berenice's English had greatly improved. When Clémence opened the door, the two were chatting a mile a minute.

"Long time, no see," Berenice said.

Clémence smiled and let them in. "I saw you this morning."

"Then you disappeared for the rest of the day. I had to make candy-cane-flavored macarons all by myself."

"Oh, I'm sure you handled it fine. It did turn out okay, didn't it?"

The candy-cane-flavored macarons were a new invention that Clémence, Berenice and Sebastien had come up with during their brainstorming sessions. Sometimes, they simply enjoyed being creative to bring new flavors of macarons to their Paris locations. If a flavor was a hit, they'd expand it to the rest of the world.

"Sebastien loved it, but Ben, not so much."

Clémence turned to Ben expectantly.

"Well, er, it's not my cup of tea," he said. "I'm a boring guy. I like classic flavors."

"He's very vanilla," Berenice teased.

"Hey, guys." Arthur entered the kitchen. "Join us in the living room for some wine."

"Ben here was just telling us how he hated our new macaron flavor," Clémence said.

"You girls are twisting my words. To tell you the truth, I don't have much of a sweet tooth."

Clémence looked at Ben in shock this time. "What? How is that possible?"

"I'm more of a savory guy."

"You don't like chocolate? Candy? Macarons?"

"I like them okay, but I don't go nuts over them like everyone else. I do like a good madeleine with my tea."

"This is the second time you mentioned tea in the span of two minutes," Berenice said. "You are so British."

Arthur handed him a glass of wine. "And here we are, drinking red wine every night. How cliché are we?"

"We'd share our baguette," Clémence joked, "but we ate it all."

All of them kicked back and joked for a while. After the day Clémence had, she appreciated the normalcy and the comfort of being around her best friends. Still, the topic of the murders couldn't be avoided.

"Your main suspect is dead?" Ben asked in disbelief.

Clémence nodded. "Jennifer Moss, Adine's business partner."

She filled Ben and Berenice in on her day's events, how she found Jennifer's body, and Cyril's theories about who killed the women.

"I'm with you," Ben said. "It's got to be someone else. Someone we're not considering."

"It *could* be Perrie," Berenice said. "The case against her does sound suspicious. I don't agree that she's in cahoots with Noel. Maybe she has motivations that you haven't uncovered yet."

"I suppose it doesn't hurt to check," Arthur said. "You've been surprised before."

"It's frustrating," Clémence said. "I was so sure it was Jennifer. I guess I got overconfident. I have to be more objective about this. I'm definitely going to talk to Noel tomorrow."

"By yourself?" Arthur asked.

"Yes. Everyone else is at work."

"No way. You're not going alone to visit someone who was just detained for murder."

"He's not the murderer," Clémence said. "He's just a heartbroken artist."

"I'll go with her," Ben said. "It's my day off. He sounds like your typical sensitive artist. I know a few of those types of guys."

"What does that mean?" Arthur asked. "The sensitive type. Are they a ticking time bomb of emotions? Are they likely to be dangerous?"

"For them to kill would be extreme," Ben said. "But I wouldn't rule it out."

Chapter 13

Through her connections, Madeleine was able to find out where Noel was that morning. She called and convinced him to meet with Clémence. As Madeleine told her later, he didn't sound too happy about it, but he ultimately agreed because he'd said he wanted to get to the bottom of the murders too.

Ben and Clémence took the Métro up to Montmartre. On the train, she told Ben what she knew about Noel from Madeleine. "Noel's from a wealthy family. His mother is a successful photographer, Claire Chevalier. Have you heard of her?"

"The name sounds familiar."

"Apparently, she mostly shoots dolls and Barbie dolls posed in scenes from gruesome historical acts."

"Oh." Realization hit Ben. "Right. I know her. She did a series about the French Revolution. I went to that show five months ago. He's her son?"

"Yup. And his father founded the second-biggest advertising firm in Paris. Noel is thirty-two now, and he began painting in his teens. He's been putting on small shows here and there for years. Are you sure you haven't heard of Noel Chevalier?"

"Noel Chevalier... maybe. There are so many artists in this city, and I've been to so many shows. It's possible I've seen his work and forgotten his name. Or that I've even met him."

"And forgotten what he looks like?" Clémence teased.

"It's entirely possible," Ben said seriously.

Clémence followed the GPS on her phone to the building. It was on the north side of Montmartre, past the touristy section. The streets were more secluded, and Clémence pointed to a plain building up ahead. "This is the studio," Clémence said. "He shares it with other painters. He rents a section of it to paint."

"I've been here," Ben said. "At least a year ago. They held a show here. There was some weird performance dance art where two sisters painted their skin green and wore a dress made out of patchy gray rags. I had no idea what that was all about."

Clémence had the access code to the front of the building, and she went in. "Noel knows we're coming at this time."

"Would you have really come alone if I hadn't offered to come?" Ben asked as the door clanged closed behind them.

"Sure. I have pepper spray."

They faced a set of double doors. Since Noel was supposed to be on the second floor, they took the stairs. When they went in, they passed artists in their workspaces painting on canvases. Clémence painted in her spare time. Her ex-boyfriend had been a prominent painter. He was currently in jail, but that was another story.

She had recently started painting more. Most of her pieces hung proudly in the Damour patisseries around Paris, and some were in people's homes. While her main job was still baking, creating new dessert recipes, and overseeing the Damour patisseries, she loved her hobby as an artist.

As she walked past the handful of artists in their moments of creation, she felt inspired to make more time to pick up her paintbrush.

Noel worked in the back corner. Clémence recognized him from a photo she'd seen of him at an event. Madeleine had shown it to her on Facebook. The photo had been taken during Paris Fashion Week the previous year. His arm had been casually draped around Adine. They'd both looked bored in a glamorous way.

"I like these," Ben whispered. He referred to the giant red canvases drying on the floor. Each one was almost as tall as her five-foot-four-inch stature. He'd completed five and was currently painting the sixth.

Each painting featured a unique anatomically correct painting of a heart over a bloody abstract background of different shades of red. The blue veins and arteries contrasted the reds, dripping down the heart, bleeding blue blood.

Noel was painting the base of his new painting furiously, splashing reds everywhere. Clémence and Ben stood back to avoid getting splashed by the paint.

It seemed rude to interrupt, so they watched until Noel paused to get more paint on his brush. Ben cleared his throat. Noel turned around.

"Bonjour." Clémence greeted him with a small smile.

It took Noel a moment to register their presence. The daze of working slowly drained from his eyes, and he returned to reality. "You're Clémence?" Noel had short black hair, and dark circles, like half moons, beneath his light-blue eyes. He looked as he did in the photo, like he was tired, bored, or both.

"Thanks for agreeing to meet with me. This is my friend Ben."

Ben smiled, but Noel only returned it with a barely there nod.

"Love the series you're working on," Ben said.

"Bleeding hearts," Noel said. "That's the title of the series. It reflects the current state of my heart: bleeding."

"It certainly reflects that," Clémence said, trying not to smile. "Losing Adine must've been hard."

"Madeleine says you can help find out who the killer is," Noel said. "So you believe me? You believe that I didn't do it?"

"I do," Clémence said without hesitation.

"Good. Because the police don't think so. Even when Jennifer was killed when I was at the station. Even when they found no evidence that I was in Adine's apartment. I haven't been since we broke up."

"I believe you," Clémence said. "I know Cyril, so it must've been rough to spend the last couple of days with him."

"You have no idea. After a while, I really started questioning whether I was a killer, that I was crazy and just lost it. But I'm not crazy, and it wasn't true. You have no idea how horrible these days have been. He did everything he could to get a confession out of me, including threatening my family. But I'm not going to confess to something I didn't do."

"I'm glad," Clémence said. "Obviously, there's someone out there with motive to kill Jennifer and Adine, but we need your help in figuring out who."

Noel sighed. He put down his paintbrush and weakly gestured to some cheap plastic chairs nearby.

Clémence sat down first, followed by Ben.

Noel plopped down and put his head in his hands. "I've been thinking about this a lot," he finally said. "I kept running it through my head. Adine and Jennifer had been doing well. Their business slowly grew throughout the years, but things were going well particularly in the last two years. The brand was getting recognized more, and they were getting more high-profile coverage in the media. I even met Adine at one of those swanky charity balls. The only thing I can think of is that whoever killed them would be someone jealous of their success."

"And who could that be?" Clémence asked. "A rival wedding designer?"

"Maybe, but I have this suspicion. It's not confirmed..."

He trailed off, prompting Ben to ask, "What is it?"

"I'm not sure Adine designed everything herself."

"You mean, there's another designer?" Clémence asked. "Why would you say that?"

"Adine was very talented. Everyone knew that. But she was also very insecure. She doubted herself, threw dozens of sketches out at a time. I guess you can say that we were very similar. That's why we didn't last. Two firecrackers caused an explosion. Anyway, she had a distinct way of drawing. I've seen it. And I've also seen design sketches that'd made it to production, and those drawings don't match up completely with Adine's style."

"So there was another designer, and Adine was taking credit for her work?"

"She never told me outright," Noel said, "and this is only my suspicion. I never questioned her about it because Adine was already touchy about her work. As an artist, I have a discerning eye, and I'm pretty sure she didn't draw some of the original sketches. That's all I know. Who knows? Maybe it was an ex-assistant who sketched out Adine's ideas, but..."

"But what?"

"I just can't see Adine doing that. She's a bit of a control freak. She wouldn't let assistants take over the creative process that way."

"So, were the drawing styles similar?" Ben asked.

"Very. To the average person, they might not even tell it's the work of different artists. But I can. Maybe Adine secretly hired someone to design for her."

"A ghost designer?" Ben asked.

"It's not unusual," Clémence said. "Perhaps this hired designer wanted more credit and killed Adine in the heat of an argument."

"Look, I don't know," Noel said. "Maybe I'm crazy like the police say. Don't take what I say as fact. Look into it yourselves."

"We will," Clémence said. "Can you tell us anything else that struck you as unusual about this whole thing, or anything that can help us?"

"Adine and Jennifer were both excited about the prospect of expanding their shop at one point. They wanted Adine to be like Vera Wang—have perfumes, a clothing line, and everything. Jennifer was gung ho about doing that. She had prospects lined up, investors, and everything, but Adine just didn't want to go through with it. She wanted to remain a small boutique until she figured things out."

"What do you mean by figure things out?"

"I don't know exactly. I heard them arguing once when I was visiting Adine in her studio, back when we were still dating."

"I don't mean to pry, but why did you break up? Was there someone else?" Clémence wondered if there had been another man in the picture.

"No. Adine was holed up in her studio all the time, trying to work. Her ambition was to become a famous designer, like mine is to be a well-known painter. I thought we would continue to work and ultimately marry and be a power couple. Well, maybe Adine was also a little envious of me. I never have problems creating new work. The pressure doesn't get to me. And for Adine, well, she started showing runway collections in the past few years, and it's a lot of pressure with the deadlines and everything, you know? We didn't break up because of another guy. We broke up because she cared more about her work than about our relationship. I tried so hard to win her back, but she couldn't stand me when she wasn't doing well creatively. Maybe she was right. Two artists in a relationship is probably trouble."

"I can attest to that," Clémence said. "My ex was an artist, and there was a bit of a competitive streak. I have to admit that in school, I was jealous of his work and felt like a total failure in comparison."

"So you dumped him?" Noel asked with an accusatory tone.

"Actually, he cheated on me."

"Oh." Noel softened. "Sorry to hear that."

"Don't feel too bad. He's in jail now. Long story. But back to this, do you have anything else you can tell me?"

"That's all I can think of. Try to find her old sketches. They're probably still in her atelier." Noel stood up, and Clémence followed.

"Thanks for your time," she said. "We'll look into it and let you know what comes of it."

"Please do. Please find Adine's killer." Noel's face conveyed everything. He still loved her. His heart must've been really bleeding.

Chapter 14

Clémence wanted to proceed with her investigation the first thing the next morning, but the holidays were coming, and her family was arriving in town. She had to pick her parents up at the Charles de Gaulle airport.

Clémence waited at the arrivals gate holding up a handwritten "Damour" sign for fun. Monsieur and Madame Damour arrived a little past eleven in the morning. They'd been living in Asia for the past year to ensure the new Damour locations in Hong Kong, Tokyo, and Singapore were successful. Her parents had to make sure the management, staff, and business practices were running smoothly in all of the Asian locations before they could return to Paris.

"Clémence, *ma puce!*" Her mother abandoned her carry-on luggage with her father as she ran to hug Clémence. Madame Damour was a lovely brunette who looked a lot like her daughter.

Clémence's father looked distinguished with salt-and-pepper hair and bright-blue eyes that she had inherited.

Since she hadn't seen her parents in months, she had offered to pick them up in the family car. Her parents' five suitcases barely fit in the trunk and backseat.

While her father was tired from his trip, her mother was as sprightly and chatty as ever. She recounted their adventures traveling around China. "They have the strangest beauty treatments. Did you know that they eat donkey hide for better skin in China? Something about increasing the collagen in your skin."

"I've never heard of that," Clémence said. "Did you try it?"

"No, but I wanted to. We went around with a translator who recommended really good restaurants, but none of them offered donkey hide. There were some specialty restaurants in Beijing, but we didn't go there. Your father didn't want to try them."

"Do you blame me?" Monsieur Damour asked. "I wanted to eat the food Xiu recommended. I don't need to eat to grow collagen or whatever it is."

"But look at all your wrinkles," Madame Damour teased.

"I like them just fine."

"I think you look rugged and very handsome, Papa," Clémence said.

"What about me?" Madame Damour took pride in her beauty.

"Your skin is like white peaches," she said.

"You're kind." Her mother pinched her on the cheek.

"Maman," Clémence whined. "I'm driving."

"You get cuter every day."

"Papa, ask Mom to stop treating me like a baby."

"Well, you're going to have to start creating babies of your own for that to happen."

Clémence rolled her eyes. "So this starts."

"What?" Madame Damour asked innocently. "Is that unreasonable? You and Arthur are getting married."

"You already have plenty of grandchildren. You're just being greedy now."

"Okay, we'll lay off," her dad said. "You're still young. You know, I read an article online that mentioned you. A friend forwarded it to me. It was about the publishing heir. The article said you had helped the police with solving the murder."

"Oh, it's true," Clémence said. "Unfortunately, I seem to get wrapped up in more crimes than

I'd like. The head inspector hates it, but I do help sometimes."

"Paris is becoming more dangerous," her mother said. "But maybe it's always been dangerous."

Clémence had helped the police solve eight cases. She was tempted to tell them about the more recent case. She decided not to so they wouldn't worry. It was the holidays after all, and they were probably more jet-lagged than they let on.

She was still concerned that the Damour products would be connected with the murders one day, but that was something she shouldn't worry about. Her parents, particularly her father, had never been too concerned about bad press. He believed any press was good press.

In the second year Damour had been open, a jealous competitor had spread a rumor in the press that Damour was using expired dairy products to save on expenses, and that their desserts were making people sick. The newspapers had a field day, but Monsieur Damour only shrugged off the claims, saying they were ridiculous. Business seemed to lag for a few days, but later on that year, they became so popular they decided to open their second location in Paris.

Although Clémence still didn't want people to think Damour products were cursed, she was prepared to deal with the public fallout should someone like Cyril start spreading that story.

"Your apartment is in pristine condition," Clémence said. "And don't worry, I'll be out of your hair as soon as Arthur and I get the keys to our new place. Well, after we buy some furniture."

"You and Arthur." Her mother smiled. "I always knew you'd hit it off. Madame Duboir and I always thought so."

"If only I fell in love with a tattooed motorcyclist instead," Clémence teased. "You would have loved that too, wouldn't you?"

Her dad chuckled. "Arthur's a smart guy. He came over with his brother once, and we all talked over glasses of scotch. He has good taste in music too."

Arthur loved his '70s rock. In many ways, he was an old man.

"You can stay with us as long as you like," her mother said. "In fact, I'll really miss you. You're the last of our children to leave home and officially start out on your own." She was getting teary eyed.

"I won't be far," Clémence reassured her. "I'm a neighborhood away."

"Yes." Her mother folded her hands in her lap. "At least you'll be in Paris. Henri and Marianne only see us on special occasions."

When they went up to the apartment, Miffy greeted them with loud, enthusiastic barks.

"*Mon chou.*" Madame Damour scooped the white dog into her arms and kissed her head. "I missed you so much. Did you miss me?"

Miffy barked.

"I think that's a yes," Monsieur Damour said.

"I'll let you settle in," Clémence said. "Henri is arriving on Wednesday, and Marianne on Thursday. I can't remember the last time we were all together in Paris like this."

"I'm glad to be home," Madame Damour exclaimed.

Chapter 15

Berenice still smelled strongly of sweet baked goods after her morning shift in the Damour kitchen. As they waited for Perrie on the side street of La Belle, Clémence smelled Berenice's neck.

"What are you doing?" Berenice asked, half laughing.

"Trying to figure out what you were making this morning."

"Well?"

"Umm, chocolate éclairs?"

"Not even close."

Perrie arrived, looking sharp in a black pantsuit.

"This is my friend Berenice," Clémence said. "Berenice, Perrie."

"You have a lot of friends." Perrie said.

"You can never have enough friends. You look smart. Did you come from a meeting?"

"Thanks," Perrie replied. "Yes, I just came from a job interview. Fingers crossed that I get it."

"What job is it?"

"It was for a cosmetics company, so not exactly fashion, but they're a good company to work for." She sighed. "It's a starting position, but at least it's not for assistant work. I would be working in the marketing department. At this point, I'll take anything that pays."

As they entered the back door to La Belle, Perrie shook her head. "It's more than enough to have one dead boss, but two? It's crazy."

"I'm so sorry," Clémence said.

"To think that there's a maniac out there killing people who work at La Belle." Her brown eyes widened as she whipped her head around to look at Clémence. "You don't think they'll come after me next, do you?"

"No," Clémence said, although she wasn't completely sure.

"What are we looking for exactly?" Perrie asked. "What kind of clues?"

"Well, I want to find out if someone has been helping Adine with any of her designs. Do you know if Adine hired someone to help her with her designs?"

Perrie shook her head. "No. She always drew alone. The seamstresses only took instructions from Adine."

"Did you ever suspect Adine of using another designer?"

"No, I don't think so. Adine probably wouldn't tell me directly, either. I've only been working for her for a month. I don't think she trusted me enough with that info when I was mainly doing coffee runs and running random errands."

The three women went upstairs to the studio.

"Did she ever consult with you about the designs?" Clémence asked.

"Not really. When she was drawing, she didn't like to be disturbed. Sometimes, I was able to take a peek when I was nearby. Personally, I thought her designs were good, but at the end of the day, I'd usually find a wastepaper basket full of rejects."

"Let's put on our gloves," Berenice said. She passed out some plastic gloves from a box in her purse. "Don't want our prints on anything."

"We're looking for Adine's sketches," Clémence said. "We want to compare the styles of the illustrations. Noel said that some of the drawings are not in her usual style. If we can find a sketch that

Adine didn't do, we might be able to track down who this other designer is, if there is one."

"Okay." Perrie nodded. She opened the door cautiously, as if she were scared a ghost might jump out and scare her.

"Hello?" Clémence yelled.

The place was still marked as a crime scene, but the police weren't there.

"All right, where did she keep her drawings?" Berenice asked Perrie.

"They were usually scattered on the tables, but she must have kept them somewhere on these shelves."

They looked through one shelf along the wall that was full of design books, boxes, binders, and picture frames.

"They're in these binders," Berenice said. "Dated by year." She passed the binders among them so they could start scrutinizing them.

"That's her signature," Perrie said, pointing to the big loopy A in the right-hand corner of each dress sketch.

Clémence had the binders for the most recent two years. As she looked through the sketches, she thought that perhaps Noel was wrong. In her eyes, the illustration styles were the same. Then she got to the last binder, from the current year. She was halfway through the illustrations before she stopped on one familiar dress design. "That's my dress," she exclaimed.

Berenice and Perrie came over and crouched down next to her.

"Look." Clémence pointed to the drawing of the familiar lace dress with the low front and the body-hugging silhouette. "This dress is from the current season, but Adine didn't design it."

"Really?" Perrie asked.

"The style is familiar. It's almost as if someone was mimicking Adine's loose drawing style, but you can tell it's someone else. This sketch is more controlled. Someone spent a lot of time on the detailing."

"Where's the signature?"

The loopy A on the top right-hand corner was missing.

Clémence looked closer. "Here. See the faint pencil mark? What does that look like to you?"

"I think it's an E," Perrie said.

"E...V," Berenice added.

"So whoever did it had the initials E.V.," Perrie said. "Who could that be?"

Before Perrie could come to that conclusion, the answer struck Clémence. She pulled out her cell phone. "I'm calling the police. I know who killed Adine and Jennifer."

Chapter 16

The police had already arrived in front of the murderer's apartment building by the time Clémence got there. She, Berenice, and Perrie decided it was faster to walk there than to take the Métro. The traffic was unpredictable because it was quite busy, and the 14th arrondissement had fewer Métro stops.

Inspector Cyril St. Clair was getting out of his tiny clown car when the girls approached. He only nodded at Clémence with the stoniest of expressions then looked away, giving terse instructions to his team.

Clémence followed Cyril and three armed policemen through the front door. Berenice and Perrie came in too, but they were a good distance behind her.

On the second floor, one of the policemen kicked open the front door to an apartment. Clémence felt the ground shake and the thin walls rattle.

"Eva Vincent," Cyril shouted. "You're under arrest for the murders of Adine Wittell and Jennifer Moss."

Eva was sitting on the couch in the living room with her laptop perched on her lap. "What?" Eva was wide eyed, staring incredulously at the uniformed men suddenly inside her home. "This is ridiculous!"

"Admit it." Clémence entered and met Eva's eyes. "You killed Adine first, in the heat of the moment, then Jennifer, when you realized she knew you were the one who'd killed Adine."

"Why would I murder friends I've worked with for years?"

Cyril cuffed Eva. "Friends?" Cyril sneered. "They were hardly your friends. They were your employers."

"We know that you've been helping Adine design a portion of her collections," Clémence said. "She'd use at least one of your designs every year."

"Search her home," Cyril said to his team. "Search for her sketches and other evidence."

"That's why you were so enthusiastic when I liked the dress I tried on," Clémence continued. "The one you recommended, remember? You designed that dress. You were thrilled that I was considering buying it." She shook her head. "It's such a shame, because it's a lovely dress."

Eva's lips quivered. "It's all I wanted to do. Design."

"And Adine gave you the chance," Clémence said.

"Yes. She was slipping. She used to be good, but every year, her designs became more and more mediocre. So she used me, knowing that I wanted to design too. She said she would give me credit, but after four years, only she got successful, and I got stuck on the sales floor. I'd had enough."

"Did you plan on killing her, or was it an accident?"

"It was an accident, but you know what? I don't regret it. Adine had it coming. She treated everyone—her assistants, her seamstresses, and me—like crap. She thought she could just pay me a hundred euros for my design, and that would be that. I deserved more than that. I deserved part ownership of her business."

"Is that why you killed Jennifer too?" Clémence asked.

"Jennifer was on Adine's side. I thought she suspected me because she was the only one who knew that Adine was using my designs. When I went to talk to her, she didn't think it was me, but she was serious about closing La Belle. This store is practically my home, and Jennifer, who wasn't even here most of the time, thought she could just close it down! Well, I showed her."

"You were practically running the store," Clémence said. "So you thought with Jennifer out of the way, you could take over."

"Yes. I had plans. I would've done a way better job than those idiots. Even though I didn't go to fashion school or have money like they did, I could have made La Belle the massive success Jennifer always wanted it to be. If only she could have seen that Adine was washed up. How could she not see how good I was? Sure, I had some satisfaction in seeing my dresses made and having the customers pay ten thousand euros or more for some of them, but Adine got all the credit. Adine, Adine, Adine!"

"How did you even do it?" Cyril asked. "Weren't you on the sales floor?"

"I took a break between appointments. Perrie was out for lunch, so it was my chance to speak to Adine alone. She said she was going to stop using my designs, and that she had no intention of revealing to anyone that I'd helped on her past collections. I got so mad that I grabbed the nearest thing I could get my hands on, and I hit her. She had no intention of helping me with my design career. It was all about making her look good. She wasn't supposed to die, but I couldn't help it. She deserved it!" Eva laughed bitterly. "And with Jennifer gone,

I would've designed the collections and managed the store, and neither of them would have gotten in the way." Eva continued to cackle as Perrie and Berenice exchanged worried glances.

"Well, I'm sorry, Eva," Clémence said. "You're going to jail for a very long time. It's a shame, because you are so talented. I won't be wearing your dress on my wedding day, no matter how beautiful it is."

Chapter 17

Not only were Clémence's parents world-renowned bakers, but they were also mean chefs as well. Their Christmas Eve meal was a feast, to say the least, and they wouldn't let their children help one bit.

"You don't even want me to help with the salad?" Marianne asked in the kitchen.

"Absolutely not," Madame Damour said. "You have little ones running around."

"That's okay. Clémence is running around with them."

"Or trying to keep up with them," Clémence called.

"And you need some rest," her mother said. "Go lie down."

"Maman, I'm pregnant, not ill."

Clémence was so happy that her brother Henri and sister Marianne were home. Henri and his wife, Ella, had two children, five-year-old David and two-year-old Helen. Helen was already speaking in sentences. They certainly had a lot of energy, and Clémence had to make sure they weren't bumping into the furniture. The Damour apartment wasn't all kid friendly.

Marianne and her husband, Michel, had three-year-old fraternal twins, a boy and a girl. They certainly had more energy and were running around the living room. Clémence kept a close eye on them because there were a lot of fragile vinyls on the lower shelves, and the twins took an interest in them until she distracted them with ring around the rosie.

Marianne was four months pregnant, so at least their parents would be distracted by the new arrival soon and get off Clémence's case about reproduction when she hadn't even tied the knot yet.

"What's it like to give birth?" Clémence asked.

Marianne laughed. "You always ask me, and you never like the answer."

"Is it that painful?"

"It's different for everyone, but for me, it was the worst. I can't explain it. You'll just have to experience it yourself."

"Looking forward to doing it again?"

"Well, in the moment, it's horrible, but when it's over, you know it was worth it."

"What about a baby being in your body?" Clémence asked. "Is it weird to have a human growing inside of you?"

"At least it's only one this time," Marianne said. "Surely, it'll be easier this time than the last. Sometimes, I get weird cravings, or my body feels too hot, or I get dizzy, but it's all part of the experience. Like I said, you'll find out when you get there."

Clémence sighed. "I'm going to be an adult soon, aren't I?"

Marianne laughed again. "What? You already are an adult."

"It feels like only yesterday we were playing together in Romainville and learning how to spell at school. I can't believe it's been years since I graduated from college. Now, I'm getting married? Thinking about having kids? It's crazy!"

"It'll be a fun ride," Marianne reassured her. "At least you've had your fun. You got to travel, work, make friends. You were single for a while too, so you could stand on your own two feet. I got married right out of college, so I couldn't do that."

"That's true. I'm lucky. And so are you."

"Oh, of course. I don't regret marrying Michel and having kids for a second. At least we traveled and had fun before we had kids. Now, whenever we go anywhere, we travel with so much stuff."

"I've seen your luggage," Clémence said. "I don't know how you do it."

"You learn how to juggle. The only luxury is alone time."

"I'll have to tell that to my friend Celine. She's single and doesn't always enjoy it."

"Tell her to appreciate it while she can. Everywhere I go, I have little ones following me around, this baby in my belly, and a grown man who's as excited about a trip to the patisserie as the kids are."

"That sounds sweet," Clémence said.

"It is." Marianne smiled. She shared Clémence's smile. For a while, as children, Marianne and Clémence looked like carbon copies of each other, but Marianne kept her hair long, usually tied in a loose bun, and she was taller and thinner, with a longer face.

"When are you going to tell me the sex of the baby?" Clémence asked.

"I don't even know," Marianne said.

"Really?"

"I want it to be a surprise. I'll only know when he or she comes out."

"I think that's what I would like to do when I have kids," Clémence said.

Marianne winked at her. "So you will be having children, then?"

"Stop." Clémence groaned.

After a delicious family dinner, everyone was too stuffed to eat dessert, even the children. Clémence had brought Damour's limited edition Christmas treats, including gingerbread, candy cane macaroons, and eggnog éclairs.

The family settled on coffee and hot chocolate after the meal. Clémence offered to make it for everyone. Her sister was allergic to dairy, so she made Marianne's hot chocolate with almond milk.

"Clémence," Henri said. "Are you still helping the police solve cases?"

"She just helped with one a few days ago," their mother said. "It's a long story involving a wedding dress boutique."

After some urging, Clémence told them everything. "Eva would've been a great designer. Too bad she was a murderer."

"You're right not to buy that dress," Ella said. "Sad to hear it's closing down, though. I had a friend who bought a dress from there."

"When did you start helping the police?" Michel asked.

"Oh, by total accident," Clémence said. "Ever since I found the gardienne's dead body downstairs when I first came back from my travels."

"That must've been a rude welcome-home surprise," Michel said.

"Tell me about it." Clémence had been trying to get the gardienne to warm up to her, but instead found the woman's cold body on the floor. The Damour macarons had been poisoned.

"Clémence did find a dress, though," her sister said. "Even though she wouldn't show it to me."

"You'll have to wait to see it at the wedding."

"Who's the designer?" Ella asked.

"Marcus Savin. He's a friend of mine, and he doesn't usually design wedding dresses, but he offered to design one for me for fun."

The doorbell rang. It was the bell from the kitchen door. Clémence stood to get the door, and Miffy trailed after her. The twins did too. She opened the door to see Arthur grinning shyly.

"Who's that?" her niece asked.

"That's Arthur," Clémence said. "He's going to be your new uncle soon. Uncle Arthur. Say hi."

"Hi, Uncle Arthur," the twins said in unison.

"Hi," Arthur replied with a grin. Before he could say anything else, the kids ran away.

He laughed. "Merry Christmas, Clémence." He kissed her on the lips then gave her a box. "It was hard to find a present for the girl who has everything."

"You shouldn't have." She opened it. It was a framed photo of Arthur smiling, posed with a fist under his chin. He'd had it taken professionally.

Clémence laughed. "As if I won't be seeing plenty of your mug when we move in together."

"You say that like it's a bad thing."

"Where's my real present?"

"I'll give you your real present tomorrow."

"Come in and meet the family. We're having hot chocolate."

Arthur came in. "You know, I always used to be able to smell your kitchen."

His family lived on the third floor, but he kept a small room on the roof to exercise his independence. "When I used to come downstairs, I would smell whatever it was that you or your family were making."

"Were you jealous?"

"I would be if our chef wasn't so good."

"Have you eaten?" Clémence asked.

"I'm so full."

"Room for dessert?"

"Always."

"Good, I have Damour goodies for you."

"You're coming over to see my family later on, aren't you?" Arthur asked.

"Of course I am," Clémence said. "We're going to need a bigger place if we ever invite all our family together under one roof."

Clémence giggled, imagining her family and Arthur's together. Arthur had six siblings.

"The place would be a madhouse," he said.

She closed the door behind him and took Arthur's arm. Together, they walked into the living room to be with her family.

Recipe #1

French Hot Chocolate

Inspired by the hot chocolate recipe from the famous Café Angelina in Paris, this dark hot chocolate recipe is intense, rich, and decadent.

Makes 2-4 cups

Ingredients:
- 1 1/2 cups whole milk
- 1/2 cup heavy cream
- 2 teaspoons powdered sugar
- 8 ounces bittersweet chocolate, at least 70% cocoa

• Giant bowl of whipped cream, for serving

In a medium saucepan over medium heat, whisk together whole milk, heavy cream, and powdered sugar until small bubbles appear around the edges. Do not allow the mixture to boil.

Remove saucepan from heat. Stir in the chopped chocolate until melted, returning the sauce to low heat if needed for the chocolate to melt completely. Serve warm, topped with lots of whipped cream.

Recipe # 2

Healthy Hot Chocolate

Makes 2 cups

Ingredients:

- 2 cups almond milk
- 4 teaspoons raw cacao
- 2 tablespoons maple syrup
- 1/2 teaspoon vanilla extract
- Pinch or two of sea salt

Combine all the ingredients into a saucepan. Stir over high heat for three minutes.

About the Author

Harper Lin is the USA TODAY bestselling author of The Patisserie Mysteries, The Emma Wild Holiday Mysteries, The Wonder Cats Mysteries, and The Cape Bay Cafe Mysteries.

When she's not reading or writing mysteries, she loves going to yoga classes, hiking, and hanging out with her family and friends.

www.HarperLin.com